語言是通往世界的橋梁

語言鳥
Parrot
語言是通往世界的橋梁

ESSENTIAL WORDS

ESSENTIAL WORDS:
ENGLISH VOCABULARY IN PRACTICE

最實用的
國民生活英語
單字書

美式發音對照
◎錄音至296頁

臧琪蕾 編著

想學英語？
就從生活基礎開始！

隨著國際化的腳步加速，你的競爭力夠嗎？
還是有限的英語能力已降低你的競爭力？
單字實力決定「聽說讀寫」的流暢度與精準度
絕對是英語語言根基的磐石

準備好跟上時代的腳步了嗎？
迫不及待跟外國人開口說英語了嗎？ GO！
◎本書錄音至296頁

前言大綱

全民英檢，大考英聽，國外出差，出遊旅行，對於英文聽説讀寫能力的挑戰已經全面性地向您席捲而來。

隨著國際化的腳步加速，您是否覺得自己的競爭力，已經因為自身有限的英語實力已備感壓力?

您是否覺得職場中，越來越無法避免與外國人士洽工商辦；抑或是您是否發覺到以前學校學到的英文，無法應付您國外旅遊的需要?

在語言學習裡，實力的養成第一步，就是單字量的多寡了。您的單字力會先決地決定你的語言聽説讀寫的流暢度與精準度。所以，單字力的養成絕對是語言利的基石。

然而，要先學會哪些單字呢？

學英文，應該要先從生活基礎開始！

針對日常生活以及國外旅行，本書規劃十八個章節最實用的生活英文主題，在這幾個單元裡，列舉了我們平常急用的基本字彙，簡附上使用説明，並以熟悉的生活對話為例句，讓您在熟悉的生活情境中記憶並活用英文日常生活中的基本字彙。而這些最常見的基本單字以及會話例句都能讓您在生活中無論是出國臨時急用，或是在國內遇到外國旅客，都能用最道地的英文與外國人應對自如，化解尷尬，讓您輕鬆跨出養成英文單字力的第一步。此外，附錄裡參考了全民英檢的常考單詞而簡附上常見的英文單詞群以及全民英檢基礎動詞的動詞變化，讓您無論是在生活應用或是準備考試，英文單字力紮實穩健。

建議您依照本書所附的真人發音的學習光碟，先學習每一個單字的正確發音，然後隨著外籍老師口語會話的頻率伴讀，熟悉單字應用生活例句，讓您增進語感與英文聽力的養成。每天跟著學習光碟大聲練習。一天一個單元練習，頂多花您10分鐘的時間，您就會發現字彙量與日俱增，口語會話的技巧更為流暢，就可以讓開口說英文變得很輕鬆了。

詞性說明

養成單字力的第一步，就是要了解字的外型。除了拼法之外，字的詞性是它在一個句子裡的外型，是非常重要的一個環節。從字到句子，我們要要先從詞性下手，下列是英文常見單詞詞性，也是本書各章節使用表示詞性的方法：

縮寫	中文詞性	原文	例字
n. [C]	可數名詞	countable noun	dog, flower
n. [U]	不可數名詞	uncountable noun	time, money
pron.	代名詞	pronoun	I, you, we
adj.	形容詞	adjective	smart, good
vt.	及物動詞	transitive verb	do, eat, have
vi.	不及物動詞	intransitive verb	sit, arrive, come
aux.	助動詞	auxiliary	can, may
adv.	副詞	adverb	well, very
conj.	連接詞	conjunction	and, or, when
prep.	介系詞	preposition	in, at, between
phr.	片語	phrase	take away, in time

第一章 基本常用字彙 Part One Basic Words

第二章 日常最急用 Part Two Daily Basics

第三章 旅行最急用 Part Three In Travelling

PART ONE BASIC WORDS

基本常用字彙

Chapter 1

person

【`pɝsn】

n. [C]（一個）人

person的複數形是people「人群，人們」。人類是human，動物則是animal。而男人是man，女人則是woman。

- people 【`pip!】 n. pl. 人群，人們
- human 【`hjumən】 n. [C] 人類
- animal 【`ænəm!】 n. [C] 動物
- man 【mæn】 n. [C] 男人 複數形是men
- woman 【`wʊmən】 n. [C] 女人 複數形是women

例句

Richard is the right person for this job.
理查是這個工作的不二人選。

You have to collect the prize in person.
你必須親自領取獎金。

會話

A: Did you read today's newspaper? Brian hit the headline.
你讀了今天的報紙嗎？布萊恩登上頭版頭條了耶。

B: Well, he is a famous person now.
是啊，他現在可是一個名人了呢。

thing

【θɪŋ】

n. [C] 事物，東西

「物體」還可以稱做object，「事情」還可以用matter來表示。

- object【`ɑbdʒɪkt】n. [C] 物體
- matter【`mætɚ】n. [C] 事情

例句

A housekeeper has to handle a lot of things.
一個管家必須要做很多事。

To say is one thing; to do is another.
說是一回事；做又是一回事。

會話

A: Would you like to go swimming with us?
你要跟我們去游泳嗎？

B: It sounds like a nice thing to do.
這件事聽起來不錯。

this

【ðɪs】

pron. 這個

this的複數形是these。that是那個，其複數形是those。如果分不出是「這個」或是「那個」，最常用的代名詞是it(表示單數)與they(表示複數)。

- these 【ðiz】 pron. 這些
- that 【ðæt】 pron. 那個 複數形是those
- it 【ɪt】 pron. 它 複數形是they

例句

This is none of your business.
這不關妳的事。

These are my pens.
這些是我的筆。

會話

A: Which cell phone do you like?
你喜歡哪一支手機？
How about this fashionable and multifunctional one?
這一支流行又多功能的手機如何？

B: This looks good.
這支看起來不錯。

mistake

【mɪˋstek】

n. [C] 錯誤，過失

同義詞有error。「問題」是problem，而「麻煩」是trouble。

- error 【ˋɛrɚ】 n. [C] 錯誤，過失
- problem 【ˋprɑbləm】 n. [C] 問題
- trouble 【ˋtrʌbl̩】 n. [C] [U] 麻煩

例句

The teacher pointed out the student's spelling mistake.
老師指出那位學生的拼字錯誤。

Don't make any mistakes.
別出差錯。

會話

A: Why do you say such insulting words to me?
你為什麼要對我說這樣傷人的話？

B: Calm down. It must be a mistake.
冷靜下來，你一定是搞錯了。

word

【wɝd】

n. [C] 字，話

letter是「字母」，phrase是「字詞」，article則是「文章」。

- letter 【`lɛtɚ】 n. [C] 字母
- phrase 【frez】 n. [C] 詞，慣用語
- article 【`ɑrtɪk!】 n. [C] 文章

例句

We learnt a lot of new words in today's English class.
我們在今天的英文課學到了好多字。

Pan left us without saying a word.
潘未留下一句話就離我們遠去。

會話

A: How do you learn English?
你是怎麼學英文的？

B: When I meet a new word, I always look it up in the dictionary.
每次我遇到一個新字，我都會查字典。

piece

【pis】

n. [C] 一張，一片，一件

a piece of...是量詞表示「一張，一片，一件…」。一張還可以說 a sheet of...，而一件可以用an article of...來表示。

■ sheet【ʃit】n. [C] 片，張
■ article【`artɪk!】n. [C]（物品）一件

例句

It is a piece of cake.
這只是一塊蛋糕。（這件事很簡單）
The vase broke into pieces.
花瓶破成碎片。

會話

A: Would you please give me a piece of paper?
可以給我一張紙嗎？
B: Here you are.
這給你。

place

【ples】

n. [C] 地方，地點

地方普遍的講法是place。「地點」是location跟spot，而「地區」是area。

- location 【lo`keʃən】 n. [C] 地點，位置
- spot 【spɑt】 n. [C] 地點
- area 【`ɛrɪə】 n. [C] 地區

例句

It is impolite to shout in a public place.
在公眾場合大叫不禮貌。
Can we have a party at your place?
我們能在你家開派對嗎？

會話

A: Have you found a new place to live?
你已經找到新的住的地方了嗎？
B: Not yet.
還沒耶。

idea

【aɪˋdiə】

n. [C] 想法，主意，點子

同義詞有thought，concept跟notion。

- thought 【θɔt】 n. [U] 想法，思維
- concept 【ˋkɑnsɛpt】 n. [C] 想法，概念
- notion 【ˋnoʃən】 n. [C] 想法，概念

例句

I have no idea.

我沒有想法。（我不知道。）

會話

A: How about going dancing with us at a club tonight?

今晚跟我們一起去夜店跳舞如何？

B: That's a good idea!

這個主意真不錯！

do

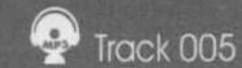

【du】

vt. 做，製作，實行

do是英文裡最常見的動詞，其動詞三態為不規則變化：do-did-done。do也可以是助動詞，用來輔助其他一般動詞形成否定句以及疑問句。

例句

Jack always does his best.
傑克總是盡全力做到最好。
The scientists did several experiments to prove their hypothesis correct.
這群科學家做許多實驗為了要證明他們的假設是正確的。
Do you know what I mean?
你知道我的意思嗎？

會話

A: Would you do me a favor?
你可以幫我一個忙嗎？
B: Sure.
當然可以。

make

【mek】

vt. 做；使…做出

在英文裡，make也是「做」的意思，強調製作。此外，make也有「使人去做…」的意思。其動詞三態為不規則變化：make-made-made。

例句

Sheldon is making tea for his guests.
謝爾頓正在為客人泡茶。

The comedian's jokes made his audience laugh.
那個喜劇演員的笑話使得他的觀眾哈哈大笑。

會話

A: What are you doing now?
你現在正在做什麼？

B: I am making cup cakes.
我正在做杯子蛋糕。

give

【gɪv】

vt. 給予，給；帶來

同義字有offer跟present。其動詞三態為不規則變化：give-gave-given。而bring也有「帶來」的意思。

- offer 【`ɔfɚ】 vt. 給予，提供
- present 【prɪ`zɛnt】 vt. 給予，贈送
- bring 【brɪŋ】 vt. 帶來 不規則變化：bring-brought-brought

例句

Our boss gave a new task to our team.
我們老闆給我們團隊一項新任務。

Your mistake gave trouble to the company.
你的失誤為公司帶來麻煩。

會話

A: Would you give me your student ID?
你可以給我你的學生證嗎？

B: Sorry, but I forgot to bring it with me.
抱歉，但我忘記帶在身上了。

take

【tek】

vt. 拿去，帶走

其動詞三態為不規則變化：take-took-taken。get是近似詞，表示「得到，獲得，收到」。

■ get【gɛt】vt. 得到，獲得，收到 不規則變化：get-got-gotten

例句

The mother took her son's hand and walked away.
這媽媽牽起了小孩的手，然後走掉了。

The waiter just took our order.
侍者剛剛才把我們的點菜單拿走。

會話

A: Did you get your Christmas present?
你拿到你的聖誕節禮物嗎？

B: Yes, it is a golden watch. My mother just took it away.
有啊，那是一隻金錶。我媽把它拿走了。

put

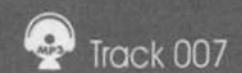

【pʊt】

vt. 放置，擺

同義詞有place跟lay。其動詞三態為不規則變化：put-put-put。

■ place【ples】vt. 放置
■ lay【le】vt. 放置 不規則變化：lay-laid-laid

例句

My father put the magazine on the desk.
我父親把雜誌放在書桌上。
Jessica put everything in order in her room.
潔西卡整齊地擺放她房間的所有東西。

會話

A: Where is my dinner?
我的晚餐在哪？
B: I put it in the refrigerator.
我把它放在冰箱了。

have

【hæv】
vt. 擁有，有

have在現在式的句子裡，如果主詞是第三人稱單數，如he，she，或it，就會變成has。其動詞三態為不規則變化：have-had-had。have/has也可以是助動詞，來輔助其他一般動詞形成完成式。

例句

Victor has a house.
維特有一間房子。
Have they reached an agreement?
她們已經達成共識了嗎？

會話

A: Do you have time?
你有時間嗎？
B: Sure. What's up?
有啊，怎麼了？

show

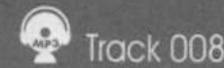

【ʃo】

vt. 顯示，指出，呈現　n. [C] 表演

當它是「呈現」的意思時，其同義字有present跟display。

- present【prɪˋzɛnt】vt. 呈現，顯示
- display【dɪˋsple】vt. 呈現，顯示

例句

Can you show me the way to the train station?
你可以向我指出往火車站的路嗎？
Please show me your permit.
請出示你的通行證。

會話

A: Please show me your identification card.
請出示你的身分證。
B: Here you are.
在這裡。

speak

【spik】

vt., vi. 說；談話

speak是說，強調「使用…語言」或是「(出聲)說…」的意思，其動詞三態為不規則變化：speak-spoke-spoken。除此之外，speak也有「向…談話」而talk雖然也是說話，談話，但是偏重「聊天」的意思。

■ talk【tɔk】 vi. 向…說話，談話；聊天
n. [C] [U] 說話，談話

例句

Do you speak Italian?
你會說義大利文嗎？

Is Julia speaking?
是茱莉亞在說話嗎？(電話用語)

會話

A: Do you speak Thai well?
你泰國話說得好嗎？

B: Yes. We can have a talk in Thai.
不錯啊。我們可以用泰文聊天。

tell

【tɛl】

vt. 告訴，說…

tell也是說，但是強調「告訴某人某件事情」的意思。其動詞三態為不規則變化：tell-told-told。say是「講，說出某件事情」的意思。其動詞三態為不規則變化：say-said-said。

■ say【se】vt. 說，講

例句

Let me tell you a story.
讓我跟你說一個故事。

I have told you!
我早就跟你說過了！

會話

A: Elisa said she would not come home tonight.
伊萊莎說她今晚可能不會回家。

B: Please tell her to call me back.
麻煩請她再回我電話。

think

【θɪŋk】

vt., vi. 想，認為；思考

think of是「想到…」；think about是「考慮…」。而常說的「我想，我認為」，在英文則可以用I think...或是I consider...來表示。其動詞三態為不規則變化：think-thought-thought。

■ consider【kən`sɪdɚ】vt., vi. 考慮；認為

例句

Think twice before you leap.
三思而後行。
I think we are running out of gas.
我想我們快沒有瓦斯了。

會話

A: What do you think of this advertisement?
你對這個廣告的看法如何？
B: I think it is just a piece of trash.
我覺得它簡直就是垃圾。

know

【no】

vt., vi 知道，了解；認識，懂得

know表示了解時，同義字有see跟understand。其動詞三態為不規則變化：know-knew-known。

- see【si】vt., vi. 懂得，看
  不規則變化：see-saw-seen
- understand【ˌʌndɚ`stænd】vt., vi. 懂得，了解
  不規則變化：understand-understood-understood

例句

Young kids can't tell right and wrong.
年輕的孩子不懂是非對錯。
Juliet and Robert have known each other for thirty years.
朱麗雅跟羅伯特已經認識三十年了。

會話

A: Our teacher has known what happened.
我們老師已經知道發生什麼事了。
B: I see.
我了解了。

ask

【æsk】

vt., vi. 詢問；要求

問問題叫做ask a question。 而片語ask for是「請求…」的意思。

■ question【`kwɛstʃən】n. [C] 問題

例句

The kid asked his teacher a question.
那個孩子向他老師一個問題。
The old lady asked for help.
那位老女士請求幫助。

會話

A: May I speak to John?
我可以跟約翰說話嗎？
B: He is not around. I will ask him to call you back.
他不在喔。他回來的時候我會叫他回電話給你。

go

【go】

vi. 離去，行走

離開的同義詞有leave。而相反詞「來到」則是come。go的動詞三態為不規則變化：go-went-gone。

- leave【liv】vt., vi. 離開 不規則變化：leave-left-left
- come【kʌm】vi. 來 不規則變化：come-came-come

例句

We saw Nancy go with her mother to the hospital.
我們看到南茜跟她媽媽去醫院。

The children went out and had fun in the playground.
孩子們走出去並且在操場玩得很開心。

會話

A: Where did you go last night?
你昨晚去哪兒了？

B: I went to the laboratory and came home at 3 am.
我去實驗室，然後清晨三點回家。

start

【start】

vt., vi. 開始，出發

「開始」同義字有begin。而相反詞「結束」則是end，「停止」是stop。

- begin【bɪˋgɪn】vt., vi. 開始，出發
  不規則變化：begin-began-begun
- end【ɛnd】vt., vi. 結束
- stop【stɑp】vt., vi. 停止

例句

After getting the loan from the bank, they started their own business.
從銀行得到貸款之後，他們開始他們的生意。

The class starts at 8 o'clock.
八點開始上課。

會話

A: How can I start this program?
我要怎麼開啟這個程式？

B: All you have to do is type in your password and press "enter".
你所要做的是就是鍵入密碼，然後按「enter」鍵。

stay

【ste】

vt., vi. 停留，留下；繼續，保持

stop是指「停止某件事，某個動作」的意思，而stay則是「停留在某處」的意思。「保持」的同義字是keep。

■ keep【kip】vt., vi. 繼續，保持

不規則變化：keep-kept-kept

例句

Jenny will go and stay with her aunt over Christmas.
珍妮會待在她阿姨那過聖誕節。

Paul still stayed awake at 4 a.m. in order to finish his assignments.
保羅為了完成作業，清晨四點還保持清醒著。

會話

A: Where are you going to stay?
你預計要待在哪裡？

B: I will stay in the hotel.
我會待在飯店裡。

change

【tʃendʒ】
vt., vi. 改變；變化

change是「改變某人事物」的意思，但是某人事物「變成…」，則要用become。

■ become【bɪˋkʌm】vi. 變成，成為
不規則變化：become-became-become

例句

The new policy changes the whole system.
這項新政策改變了這個體制。

Alice changed her mind.
愛麗絲改變心意了。

會話

A: You have changed a lot.
你變好多喔。

B: Well, I think I just became a whole new person.
是啊，我想我變成一個全新的人了。

borrow

【`baro】

vt. 借，借入

borrow是借入某物的意思，而lend則是將某物借出給某人。歸還則是return。

- lend 【lɛnd】 vt. 借，借出 不規則變化：lend-lent-lent
- return 【rɪ`tɝn】 vt. 歸還

例句

How many books do you borrow from the library?
你從圖書館借了多少書出來？

Nick borrows some ideas from Sam.
尼克從山姆那借用了些想法。

會話

A: May I borrow some money from you?
我可以跟你借些錢嗎？

B: Sure, if you return the money I lent you last time.
好啊，只要你還我上次借你的錢。

apologize

【ə`paləˌdʒaɪz】

vi. 道歉

「對不起」除了I am sorry之外，還有apologize這一個動詞可以表示歉意。forgive則是「原諒」。pardon本意也是原諒，但是現在常用在口語中表示「不好意思」，跟excuse me意近。

- forgive 【fɚ`gɪv】 vt. 原諒
  不規則變化：forgive-forgave-forgiven
- pardon 【`pardn】 vt. 原諒
- excuse 【ɪk`skjuz】 vt. 原諒

例句

Owen apologized for being late this morning.
歐文為今天早上遲到道歉。

I apologize to you for hurting your feelings.
我很抱歉傷了你的感情。

會話

A: Honey, I bought you dinner to apologize.
親愛的，我買晚餐來向你道歉。

B: Well, you are forgiven.
好吧，你被原諒了。

choose

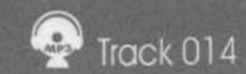

【tʃuz】

vt., vi. 選擇，挑選

同義字有select跟pick，而「決定」則是decide。choose動詞三態為不規則變化：choose-chose-chosen。

- select【sə`lɛkt】vt. 挑選
- pick 【pɪk】vt. 挑選

例句

Amy chose a necktie as a present for Samuel.
愛咪選了一條領帶給山姆當禮物。

Some people choose to commit suicide when they do not know how to solve problems.
有些人不知道如何解決問題時，會選擇自殺。

會話

A: Do you have an idea for our date on the weekend?
你對我們周末的約會有任何想法嗎？

B: How about choosing a film in the rental shop together and then watching it in your place?
要不然我們一起去電影出租店挑片，然後去你家看？

want

【want】

vt., vi. 想，想要

「想要」還有一個近似詞是wish，但wish不只是想要，更有「希望；祝福」的意思。hope也是「希望」。

- wish 【wɪʃ】 vt., vi. 想要，希望，但願
- hope【hop】vt., vi. 希望

例句

The mother wants her daughter to run errands for her.
這媽媽想要她女兒為她跑腿。

I want to take a rest.
我想要休息。

會話

A: Do you want your hair cut or permed?
你想要剪髮或是燙髮？

B: I just want to have my hair cut.
我只想要剪髮。

see

【si】

vt., vi. 看見，看到；了解

英文看有三種：see偏向短暫地看見，look則是注視，watch則是持續性地看或觀賞的意思。see動詞三態為不規則變化：see-saw-seen。

- look 【lʊk】 vi. 看
- watch 【watʃ】 vt., vi. 看，觀賞

例句

Miranda saw Roe chatting with another girl.
米蘭達看到羅伊跟別的女生聊天。

I can't see your point.
我不了解你的論點。

會話

A: How nice to see you again.
再次見到你真開心啊。

B: Nice to see you, too.
我也很開心再見到你。

good

【gʊd】

adj. 好的，有益的，善良的

同義詞有great跟nice，其相反詞是bad。good為不規則變化：good-better-best。

- great【gret】adj. 優秀的，偉大的
- nice【naɪs】adj. 好的，好心的
- bad【bæd】adj. 壞的，不好的，有害的

不規則變化：bad-worse-worst

例句

Parker is a good salesperson.
派克是一個好的銷售員。

Bananas are good for your health.
香蕉對你健康有益。

會話

A: How do you like this book?
你覺得這本書如何？

B: I think it is generally good.
我覺得它大致上良好。

many

【`mɛnɪ】

adj. 許多的，多的

同義詞是various，要注意的是many只能修飾可數名詞複數。要修飾不可數名詞則要用much。「一些」是some跟several。

- various 【`vɛrɪəs】 adj. 許多的
- much 【mʌtʃ】 adj. 許多的
- some 【sʌm】 adj. 一些
- several 【`sɛvərəl】 adj. 一些，數個

例句

Eunice has many new ideas.
優妮絲有許多新想法。

Bennett has as many tasks as Mike does.
班奈特跟麥克有一樣多的任務。

會話

A: May I take your order?
我可以幫您點餐了嗎？

B: Not yet. There are too many choices. It is hard for me to decide.
還沒。這有好多選擇，我很難做決定。

little

【`lɪtl̩】

adj. 少許，少的

要注意，little只能修飾不可數名詞，表示「很少、很少」。修飾可數名詞複數，表示很少，要用few。而a little跟a few指的是「一些」。

- few【fju】adj. 很少，幾乎沒有
- a few adj. phr. 一些

例句

I brought little money today.
我今天沒帶什麼錢。

We've got a little time before the train leaves.
在火車離開之前，我們還有一點時間。

會話

A: Greg, you look drunk!
葛瑞格，你看起來醉了！

B: But I just had a little alcohol.
但我沒有喝什麼酒啊。

every

【`ɛvrɪ】

adj. 每一個的

同義字是each。any是「任何一個的」。要注意every跟each其後接單數名詞，而any之後接單數或是複數名詞皆可。

- each【itʃ】adj. 每一個的，各自的
- any 【`ɛnɪ】adj. 任何一個的

例句

Every one has to shoulder his own responsibility.
每個人都應該要肩負自身的責任。

This convenience store is open every day.
這間便利商店每一天都營業。

會話

A: How do you lose weight?
你怎麼減肥的？

B: I work out for 2 hours every evening.
我每天傍晚運動兩小時。

real

【`riəl】

adj. 真的；確實的，實際的

當real當「真的」的時候，同義詞是true，反義詞是fake。而當real當「確實的」的時候，同義詞是actual。

- true 【tru】 adj. 真實的
- fake 【fek】 adj. 假的
- actual 【`æktʃʊəl】 adj. 實際的，事實上的

例句

What I said is real.
我說的是真的。
A real leather bag is more expensive than an artificial one.
一個真皮的包包會比人造皮的來得貴。

會話

A: Is it real that they got divorced?
他們離婚是真的嗎？
B: Yes, the news is true.
是的，這個消息是真的。

different

【`dɪfərənt】

adj. 不同的

反義詞是similar「相似的」跟same「相同的」。

- similar 【`sɪmələ˞】 adj. 相似的
- same 【sem】 adj. 相同的，同一的

例句

Everyone should respect different opinions.
每一個人都要尊重不同意見。

You are so different from how you looked ten years ago.
你跟十年前看起來不一樣。

會話

A: Emma and Eve are twins. No wonder they look alike.
愛馬跟伊娃是雙胞胎。難怪他們看起來很像。

B: But they have different ideas.
但是他們有不同的想法。

strange

【strendʒ】

adj. 奇怪的；陌生的

當strange是「奇怪」的意思時，同義詞有unusual跟uncommon。而反義字「普通的，常見的」則是common。

- unusual 【ʌn`juʒʊəl】 adj. 不平常的，奇特的
- uncommon 【ʌn`kamən】 adj. 不尋常的
- common 【`kamən】 adj. 普通的，常見的

例句

Everything in this foreign country is strange to me.
在各個異國的每一個東西，對我而言都很奇怪。

It is strange that our manager was late for work this morning.
我們經理今天早上上班遲到，真是奇怪。

會話

A: Did you sleep well last night?
你昨晚睡得好嗎？

B: No, I had a strange dream last night.
不好，我昨晚做了一個奇怪的夢。

right

【raɪt】

adj. 對的，適當的；正確的

「正確的」同義詞是correct；而「適當的」同義詞是proper。而反義詞則是wrong。

- correct【kə`rɛkt】adj. 正確的
- proper【`prɑpɚ】adj. 適當的
- wrong【rɔŋ】adj. 錯誤的，不當的

例句

Is this the right way to the gallery?
這是去畫廊對的路上嗎？

Please give me a right answer.
請給我正確答案。

會話

A: Would it be all right to have some sugar in your latte?
你拿鐵裡加點糖行嗎？

B: That's OK.
那沒關係。

dangerous

【`dendʒərəs】

adj. 危險的，不安全的

同義詞是risky，而相反詞是safe。

- risky【`rɪskɪ】adj. 危險的，冒風險的
- safe【sef】adj. 安全的

例句

It is dangerous to jaywalk in a busy street.
在繁忙的街道上橫越馬路很危險。
Smoking is dangerous to your health.
抽菸危害你的健康。

會話

A: You just ran through a red light. It's dangerous!
你剛闖了紅燈。這很危險耶！
B: Sorry. I promise I will never do that again.
抱歉，我下次不會再這樣了。

hard

【hard】

adj. 困難的；努力的　adv. 努力地

「困難的」同義詞是difficult。而easy表示「簡單的；輕鬆的」。

- difficult【`dɪfə,kəlt】adj. 艱難的，難以處理的
- easy【`izɪ】adj. 簡單的；輕鬆的

例句

Maria is a hard worker.
瑪麗亞是一個努力的員工。
It is hard to get a satisfactory job.
要取得一個滿意的工作很難。

會話

A: Why did Wilber come back to Taiwan?
為什麼威爾伯要回台灣？
B: He had a hard time working in China.
他在大陸過得很辛苦。

public

【`pʌblɪk】

adj. 公共的，眾所周知的

「私人的，私底下的」是private。

■ private【`praɪvɪt】adj. 個人的，私人的；私立的

例句

Fanny went to a public school.
芬妮上的是公立學校。
Don't litter in public places.
不要在公眾場合亂丟垃圾。

會話

A: Is there any good place for me to prepare for exams?
有什麼好地方可以讓我準備考試？
B: How about the public library?
那間公立圖書館如何？

very

【`vɛrɪ】

adv. 很，非常

表示加強語氣用，可以修飾原級形容詞跟副詞。常見同義詞有 pretty，terribly，badly。

- pretty 【`prɪtɪ】 adv. 很，非常
- terribly 【`tɛrəb!ɪ】 adv. 很，非常
- badly 【`bædlɪ】 adv. 很，非常

例句

English is very easy.
英文很容易。

Thank you very much.
真是感謝你。

會話

A: You don't look well. Are you OK?
你看起來不是很好。你怎麼了？

B: My stomach hurts very much.
我的胃好痛。

well

【wɛl】

adv. 很好地；相當地

其副詞程度變化是不規則：well-better-best。要表示某件事做得還不錯，我們可以說well-done。well的反義詞是poorly，badly。

- better 【`bɛtɚ】 adv. 更；更好地
- best 【bɛst】 adv. 最；最好地
- poorly 【`pʊrlɪ】 adv. 不好地，拙劣地
- badly 【`bædlɪ】 adv. 不好地，拙劣地

不規則變化是：badly-worse-worst

例句

The student performed quite well in this interview.
這個學生在這次面試表現良好。

Peter gets along well with his colleagues.
彼得跟他的同事相處得很好。

會話

A: You speak English very well.
你英文說得很好。

B: Thank you.
謝謝。

so

【so】

adv. 非常；如此；因此

so是一個常用的副詞。它可以修飾程度，像是so nice(非常好)；也可以代替動作，像是I think so(我也是這樣想)；甚至還可以表示「因此」。

例句

Why do you come home so late?
你為什麼那麼晚回家？

The restaurant is so noisy.
這間餐廳非常嘈雜。

會話

A: What makes you so happy?
　是什麼讓你那麼高興？

B: I just hit the jackpot!
　我剛中頭彩了！

even

【`ivən】

adv. 甚至；(用於比較級前)甚至更

even也是加強語氣的副詞。特別的是它可以修飾比較級形容詞或副詞。

例句

Jane is multilingual. She can even speak Russian.
珍會說多種語言。她甚至會說俄國話。

Although Tommy is lazier than his sister, he is even smarter than her.
雖然湯米比她姊姊懶惰，但是他卻比他姊姊聰明的多。

會話

A: Are you ready to go?
你準備好要走了嗎？

B: Not yet. I haven't even decided what to wear.
還沒。我甚至還沒決定好要穿什麼。

still

【stɪl】

adv. 還，仍舊；然而；(用於比較級前)甚至更

still的意思很多，要注意它跟even一樣可以修飾比較級形容詞或副詞。

例句

The police still could not find the missing boy.
警方仍然沒有找到那個失蹤的男孩。

It will be still colder tomorrow.
明天會更冷的多。

會話

A: Are you still looking for a job?
你還在找工作嗎？

B: No. I am a travel agent now.
沒有了，我現在是旅行社業務。

too

【tu】

adv. 很…，太…；而且，也

too是加強語氣的副詞，可以跟to並用來強調「太…以致於不能…」的句型。此外too也可以表示「還有，也」的意思。

例句

If you drink too much coffee at night, you will have trouble sleeping.
如果你晚上喝太多咖啡，你會睡不著。
Jimmy is too short to reach the cabinet.
吉米太矮以致於碰不到櫥櫃。

會話

A: I am so hungry.
我好餓喔。
B: Me, too.
我也是。

over

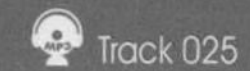

【`ovɚ】

adv. 太…；在…之上；超過…　adj. 終結，完了

over當副詞跟too一樣可以加強語氣，表示是「太…」。

例句

Calvin waited for his girlfriend for over thirty minutes.
凱爾文等他女友等了超過30分鐘。

The game is over.
比賽結束了。

會話

A: The math problem is very complicated.
這個數學題非常複雜。

B: Yeah, I think about it over and over again but I still can't figure it out.
是啊，我再三思索，但是還是想不出答案。

merely

【`mɪrlɪ】

adv. 只是，僅僅

表示語氣「只不過」。同義詞有simply，only，just。

- simply 【`sɪmplɪ】 adv. 只不過
- only 【`onlɪ】 adv. 只是，僅僅
- just 【dʒʌst】 adv. 只是

例句

Betty is merely a child.
貝蒂只是一個小孩。
It is merely a matter of time.
這只是時間的問題。

會話

A: Where can I put my luggage in the train station?
這車站哪裡可以讓我放行李？
B: You can store your luggage in one of our lockers. It merely costs you 10 dollars as a deposit.
你可以把行李存放在我們的置物櫃內。一次押金十元。

however

【hau`ɛvɚ】

adv. 然而

however是用來修飾句子並表示轉折語氣的副詞。同義詞有still，yet，nevertheless，nonetheless。

- yet 【jɛt】 adv. 然而，但是
- nevertheless 【,nɛvɚðə`lɛs】 adv. 然而，但是
- nonetheless 【,nʌnðə`lɛs】 adv. 然而，但是

例句

Dean enjoys reading. However, his sister likes to go camping.
狄恩喜歡閱讀；然而，他姐姐喜歡去露營。

Cindy studied hard for the exam; however, she failed it in the end.
辛蒂很努力地準備考試；但是，她最後還是沒考好。

會話

A: Why did Kevin and Kathy break up?
為什麼凱文跟凱西分手了？

B: Kevin is smart. However, he is very arrogant, so Kathy decided to leave him.
凱文很聰明，但是他卻很自負，所以凱西決定離開他。

also

【`ɔlso】

adv. 也

同義詞還有besides，too，as well。

- besides【bɪ`saɪdz】adv. 也
- as well adv. 也

例句

Sandy has been to Berlin, and I have also been there.
珊蒂去過柏林，我也去過。

Sean not only ate chicken but also had pork for dinner.
尚恩晚餐不只吃了雞肉還吃了豬肉。

會話

A: Is Jay a popular singer?
傑是很受歡迎的歌手嗎？

B: Yes. He is famous not only in Taiwan but also in China.
是啊，他不只是在台灣有名，在大陸也很有名。

again

【ə`gɛn】

adv. 再，再一次

同義詞是once more。

例句

Would you say that again?
請你再說一遍好嗎?

Ben got into trouble again.
班又惹禍上身了。

會話

A: Hi, this is Mary speaking.
嗨，我是瑪莉。

B: What's your name again, please?
你叫什麼名字可以再說一次嗎？

once

【wʌns】

adv. 一次；曾經

當once是「曾經」的意思，句子時態要用過去式。同義詞是one time。at once是「立刻、馬上」的意思。

例句

Emily has been to India once.
愛蜜莉去過印度一次。
They were once lovers, but now they are no longer seeing each other.
他們曾經是情侶，但是現在他們不再見了。

會話

A: How often do you go to see a movie?
你多常去電影院看電影？
B: About once a month.
大概每月一次吧。

around

【ə`raʊnd】

adv. 大約；在附近

around可以當作地方副詞表示在附近或四周的意思。當它用來表示「大約、大概」，有同義詞about，roughly，approximately。

- about 【ə`baʊt】 adv. 大約，大概
- roughly 【`rʌflɪ】 adv. 大約，大概
- approximately 【ə`prɑksəmɪtlɪ】 adv. 大約，大概

例句

There were around thirty workers in the factory.
工廠裡大約有三十名員工。

Zoe is around your age.
柔伊的年齡跟你差不多。

會話

A: How long does it take to Taitung by train?
坐火車去台東要多久時間？

B: The trip will take around six hours.
車程會需要約六小時。

therefore

【`ðɛr,for】

adv. 因此

therefore是用來修飾句子並表示因果關係的副詞。同義詞有so，thus，hence。

- thus 【ðʌs】 adv. 因此
- hence 【hɛns】 adv. 因此

例句

I think, therefore I am.
我思故我在。
It rained heavily this afternoon; therefore, the fair was cancelled.
今天下午雨下的很大；因此，園遊會就取消了。

會話

A: Why did Jamie not work in that company?
為什麼傑咪沒有在那間公司上班了？
B: She didn't work hard. Thus, she was fired.
她因為沒有努力工作；因此，她被解雇了。

moreover

【mor`ovə-】

adv. 除此之外

moreover是用來修飾句子並表示「除此之外，還有…」的副詞。同義詞有besides，still，furthermore，in addition。

- furthermore【`fɝðə-`mor】adv. 除此之外
- in addition adv. phr. 除此之外

例句

Tomatoes are nutritious; moreover, they are delicious.
番茄營養；而且很好吃。

Lisa is a teacher; moreover, she is an artist.
麗莎是一位老師，而且還是一位藝術家。

會話

A: Will you go shopping with us?
你要跟我們去逛街嗎？

B: No. I have work to do; moreover, I am running out of money.
不要，我有工作要做；而且，我錢快用完了。

always

【`ɔlwez】

adv. 總是

修飾動作發生的頻率百分之百，同義詞有all the time跟constantly。

- all the time adv. phr. 總是，一直
- constantly【`kɑnstəntlɪ】adv. 總是，一直

例句

My boss is always picking on me.
我老闆總是挑剔我。
My mother always stays at home at night.
我媽媽晚上總待在家。

會話

A: What do you think of Athena?
你覺得雅典娜如何？
B: She is remote. She always brushes me off.
她很有距離感，而且她都不理我。

often

【`ɔfən】

adv. 經常，往往

通常(動作發生頻率約百分之八十)是usually，而經常(動作發生頻率約百分之八十)則是often。同義詞有frequently，time and again。

- frequently【`frikwəntlɪ】adv. 經常，往往
- time and again adv. 經常，往往

例句

You should often comb your hair.
你應該常梳頭。
Maggie often visits her friends.
瑪姬時常去拜訪朋友。

會話

A: How often do you work out?
　你多久做一次運動。
B: I go jogging twice a week.
　我每周會慢跑兩次。

sometimes

【ˋsʌm,taɪmz】

adv. 有時候

sometime是時間副詞，表示「某天、有一天」，而sometimes是頻率副詞，表示「偶爾，有時」，同義詞有at times，once in a while，every now and then，on occasion，occasionally。

- occasion【əˋkeʒən】n. [C] 場合
- occasionally【əˋkeʒən!ɪ】adv. 有時候

例句

Everyone may sometimes make mistakes.
人有時會犯錯。

The Changs eat out on weekends sometimes.
張家人有時候周末會外出吃飯。

會話

A: How's your school life?
你學校生活如何？

B: It's fine, but sometimes I find it hard to communicate with my homeroom teacher.
還不錯，但是我覺得有時候我很難跟我導師溝通。

seldom

【`sɛldəm】

adv. 很少，不常，幾乎不

seldom是否定的頻率副詞，即not often。同義詞有hardly，rarely，barely。

- hardly【`hardlɪ】adv. 幾乎不，不常
- rarely【`rɛrlɪ】adv. 幾乎不，很少
- barely【`bɛrlɪ】adv. 幾乎不，很少

例句

It seldom rains in a desert.
沙漠幾乎不下雨。

Conservative people seldom reveal their emotions.
保守的人幾乎不顯露他們的情感。

會話

A: Oh my, I've gained three kilograms this month.
天哪，我這個月重了三公斤。

B: You seldom exercise and often eat a lot. No wonder you become heavier.
你幾乎不運動，而且又常吃很多東西。難怪你會變重。

never

【`nɛvɚ】

adv. 從未；決不

never是否定的頻率副詞，即not ever。ever是副詞，用來加強語氣表示「從來，至今」的意思。never的同義詞有in no way跟on no occasion。

例句

Lily has never been late.
麗麗從來沒有遲到過。

I have never thought of that.
我從來都沒有那樣想過。

會話

A: I want to learn Spanish, but I think I am too old.
我想學西班牙文，但是我想我太老了。

B: It is never too late to learn. Just go for it!
學習永遠不嫌遲。做就對了！

almost

【`ɔl,most】

adv. 幾乎，差不多

用來加強語氣，表示程度上「差不多」，同義詞有about跟nearly。

■ nearly【`nɪrlɪ】adv. 幾乎，差不多

例句

Debra is almost sixty now.
德布拉幾乎要六十歲了。

The car almost hit the train.
那輛車幾乎要撞上火車了。

會話

A: Today is Mom's birthday. Did you prepare any gift for her?
今天是媽媽的生日。你有準備任何禮物給她嗎？

B: I almost forgot it. Thank you for reminding me.
我差點忘了。謝謝你提醒我。

there

【ðɛr】

adv. 那裡

there是地方副詞，表示距離說話者較遠的某處「那裡」。here是地方副詞，表示距離說話者較近的某處「這裡」。there跟be動詞形成常見的句型there is/are N，表示「(某處)有…」。

■ here【hɪr】adv. 這裡

例句

You can sit there.
你可以在那裡坐。
There are five kids playing in the playground.
有五個小孩在操場玩。

會話

A: Is there anything you want to buy?
有任何你想要買的東西嗎？
B: Well, nothing in particular. I am just looking.
呃，沒什麼特別要買的，我只是看看逛逛。

enough

【ə`nʌf】

adv. 充分地；相當，很　adj. 足夠的，充足的

enough當副詞，主要是用來修飾程度上的足夠。

例句

That college student is old enough to handle everything by himself.
那個大學生已經夠大到能獨自處理任何事情。
We don't have enough time to prepare for the banquet.
我們沒有足夠的時間準備晚宴。

會話

A: I haven't seen Sarah for a while. Have you heard from her?
我好一陣子沒有看到莎拉了。你有聽說她的消息嗎？
B: Yes, she is a mother now and the baby keeps her busy enough.
有啊。她現在當媽了，而且她的寶寶也真夠她忙的了。

surely

【`ʃʊrlɪ】

adv. 確實，當然，一定

其同義詞有absolutely與of course。相反詞是perhaps跟maybe。

- absolutely 【`æbsə,lutlɪ】 adv. 當然，一定
- of course adv. 當然
- perhaps 【pə`hæps】 adv. 或許，也許
- maybe 【`mebɪ】 adv. 或許，也許

例句

Your body language surely shows your true emotion.
你的肢體語言一定會反映出你真實的情感。

Politicians surely cannot go to dinner with cash gifts.
政治人物一定不可以參加附贈禮金的餐會。

會話

A: Vincent just broke my smart phone and messed up my room!
文森摔壞了我的智慧型手機，還把我房間弄亂！

B: He is surely a jackass.
他真是個混蛋。

and

【ænd】

conj. 和，及， 與；而且；然後

and是很好用的連接詞，可以連接同詞性的字詞，也可以連結兩個相關連的句子。要注意的是連接的字跟句子語氣要相近。

例句

My friends and I are planning to go to Korea.
我朋友和我正計畫去韓國。
He opened the door, turned on the light, and sat on the sofa.
他開了門，開了燈，然後坐在沙發上。

會話 1

A: What do you like to eat?
你喜歡吃什麼?
B: I like Italian food and French food.
我喜歡義大利菜與法國菜。

會話 2

A: How do I get to the train station?
火車站怎麼走?
B: Go straight, and you will see it on your left.
直直走，然後你就會看到它在你左手邊。

but

【bʌt】

conj. 但是，可是；而是

but跟and一樣是很好用的連接詞，可以連接同詞性的字，也可以連結兩個相關連的句子。要注意的是連接的字跟句子語氣要相反相異。

例句

It is hot today, but Alice wears a sweater.
今天天氣炎熱，可是愛麗絲卻穿著毛衣。

That is not a dog but a cat.
那不是一隻狗，而是一隻貓。

會話 1

A: Would you please help me with this task?
你可以幫忙我做個任務嗎？

B: I can help you, but you have to wait for a moment.
我可以幫你，但是你要先等一下。

會話 2

A: Jennifer looks quite young.
珍妮看起來真年輕。

B: Yeah, she looks young, but actually she is in her 50s.
是啊，她是看起來很年輕，但是實際上她已經五十幾歲了。

or

【ɔr】

conj. 或者；否則，要不然

可以連接同詞性的字，也可以連結兩個相關連的句子的好用連接詞除了前面介紹的and（和）以及but（但是）之外，還有一個or。

例句

Do you like tea or coffee?

你要茶還是咖啡?

Get up, or you will be late for school.

起床了，否則你會上學遲到了。

會話 1

A: Is Kevin a doctor or a nurse?
　凱文是醫生還是護士啊？

B: He is a nurse.
　他是一位護士。

會話 2

A: Do you have any plans for this weekend?
　你這周末有什麼計畫嗎?

B: I will either go to the movies or watch TV at home.
　我要不是去看電影不然就是在家看電視。

because	so
【bɪ`kɔz】 conj. 因為	【so】 conj. 所以

「因為…，所以…」是我們說中文時為了要表示因果習慣的用語。但是在英文裡，因為一個連接詞就可以連接兩個句子，所以當我們想要用英文表示「因為…，所以…」，只要選擇because或者是so其中一個連接詞用即可。

例句

He takes a day off because he catches a cold.
他今天休息是因為他感冒了。
Lily works hard so she gets promoted.
麗麗工作辛勤，所以她升職了。

會話

A: Why are you late for work today?
你今天上班為什麼遲到？
B: I was late because the train was delayed this morning.
我遲到是因為今天早上火車誤點。

although　but

【ɔl`ðo】
conj. 雖然；儘管

【bʌt】
conj. 但是，可是；而是

「儘管雖然…，但是…」是我們說中文時為了要表示語氣轉折的用語。但是跟上一個單元介紹的一樣，在英文裡，因為一個連接詞就可以連接兩個句子，所以當我們想要用英文表示「儘管雖然…，但是…」，只要再although跟but裡擇一使用就好了。

例句

Although Henry is a little boy, he has to support his family.
雖然亨利只是一個小男孩，但是他卻必須要養家。
Olivia did not feel well, but she still finished her project on time.
雖然奧利維亞身體不舒服，但是她還是準時地完成了她的作業。

會話

A: What do you think about Tom?
你覺得湯姆如何？
B: I don't like him.
我不喜歡他。
Although he is kind to people around him, he is not smart.
雖然他對周遭的人很友善，但是他卻不聰明。

when	while
【hwɛn】 conj. 當…的時候	【hwaɪl】 conj. 當…的時候；和…同時

當我們要表明某件事是在某個時間發生時，我們可以用when連接兩個句子。while也可以連結兩個句子表明時間，只是while還有強調兩個句子的發生是在同一個時間。

例句

When I was a child, I liked to go to visit my grandparents.
在我小時候，我喜歡去拜訪我的阿公阿媽。
I will take care of everything here while you are away.
當你不在的時候，我會好好照料這裡的一切。

會話

A: When did Mary come to the office?
瑪莉什麼時候到辦公室？
B: I don't know the exact time.
我不清楚確切的時間。
She arrived here while I was having a meeting.
她到這裡時，我正在開會。

before / after

【bɪ`for】
conj. 在…之前

【`æftɚ】
conj. 在…之後

當我們要表明時間點，除了上一個單元的when跟while可以用來表示「…的時候」，還有before跟after可以來連接兩個句子，表明事情發生時間點是「在…之前」或是「在…之後」。

例句

Before Mike went to the office, he just had a cup of coffee.
在麥克去上班前，他只喝了杯咖啡。

Everyone went home after the party ended.
在宴會結束後，大家都各自回家了。

會話

A: Did you call me after you went home?
你回家後有打電話給我？

B: No, I called you when I was in the office.
不，我在辦公室的時候就打電話給你了。

until

【ən`tɪl】

conj. 直到…時，到…為止

until這一個連接詞也是用來表示時間點，不過它是用來表示某個動作或事情持續到某個時間點為止。

例句

Katy didn't go to bed until her husband went home.
直到丈夫回家，凱蒂才上床睡覺。

Jason kept playing on-line games until he felt tired.
傑森玩線上遊戲到他覺得累為止。

會話 1

A: When will the train 331 arrive?
火車331號什麼時候到？

B: The train 331 will not arrive until it is 3:45.
火車331號要到三點四十五分才會到站。

會話 2

A: Mom, may I go outside and play?
媽，我可以出去玩嗎？

B: No, you have to stay in your room until you finish your homework.
不可以，直到你寫完功課前你都要待在房間裡。

who

【hu】

pron. 什麼人，誰

當我們要問關於「誰」、「什麼人」的問題時，句子前要冠上疑問詞who。

例句

Who is Peter?
彼得是誰？

He is John's brother.
他是約翰的弟弟。

會話 1

A: Who are you calling?
你要打電話給誰？

B: I am calling Sally.
我要打電話給莎莉。

會話 2

A: Who is your new teacher?
誰是你的新老師？

B: Sam.
山姆。

what

【hwat】

pron. 什麼東西、什麼事

當我們要問關於「什麼東西」、「什麼事」等問題時，句子前要冠上疑問詞what。

例句

What is this?
這是什麼？
This is a watch.
這是一支錶。

會話 1

A: What day is today?
今天星期幾？
B: Today is Friday.
今天星期五。

會話 2

A: What's the matter with you?
你今天怎麼了？
B: I was fired.
我被炒魷魚了。

what if

假使…呢？／若是…會如何？

當我們要問關於某件事「假如」怎樣，之後又會如何等問題時，句子前要冠上疑問詞what if。

例句

What if it rains tomorrow?
要是明天下雨怎麼辦？
What if the world ended now?
要是世界現在終結了呢？

會話

A: What if we moved the shelf over there, would it look better?
如果我們把櫃子移到那兒，會比較好看嗎？
B: No, I don't think so.
不會耶，我不覺得。

which

【hwɪtʃ】

pron. 哪一個？，哪一些？

當我們要問一堆東西或是一群人中「哪一個」，「哪一些」的問題時，句子前要冠上疑問詞which。

例句

Which is my seat?
哪一個是我的座位？
This one.
這一個。

會話 1

A: Which school do you go to?
你唸哪一所學校？
B: I go to a public school in my neighborhood.
我唸在我家附近的一間公立學校。

會話 2

A: Which skirts do you like?
你喜歡哪一件裙子？
B: The red ones.
紅色那件。

where

【hwɛr】

pron. 哪裡？，何處？

當我們要某一個人，東西，或是建築在「哪裡」，「何處」時，句子前要冠上疑問詞where。

例句

Where are you going?
你要去哪裡？
I am going to the office.
我要去上班。

會話1

A: Where are you from?
你來自哪裡？
B: I am from Taiwan.
我來自台灣。

會話2

A: Where did he park his car?
他把車停哪兒？
B: He parked his car in front of the post office.
他把車停在郵局前面。

when

【hwɛn】

pron. 什麼時候？，何時？

當我們要詢問某件事情的時間點，關於「何時」，「什麼時候」的句子前要冠上疑問詞when。

例句

When were you born?
你何時生日？
I was born on May 30th.
五月三十號。

會話 1

A: When will the meeting start?
會議什麼時候開始？
B: It will begin at 8:30.
八點三十。

會話 2

A: When did the party end last night?
昨晚宴會什麼時候結束？
B: It ended at 11 o'clock.
十一點。

why

【hwaɪ】

adv. 為什麼？，為何？

當我們要詢問某件事情的原因或理由，句子前要冠上疑問詞why。

例句

Why did you leave early yesterday?
你昨天為什麼提早離開？

I felt ill so I left early.
我不舒服，所以我提早離開。

會話 1

A: Why don't you have some seafood?
你為什麼不吃些海產？

B: I am allergic to it.
我對海鮮過敏。

會話 2

A: Why did the boss get angry?
為什麼老闆生氣？

B: That's because Susan failed to finish the project on time.
那是因為蘇珊沒有準時完成計畫。

why not

為什麼呢?；何不，或…不好嗎？

當我們要反問「這樣做，不好嗎？」或是表示建議時，我們可以回問：Why not?或是Why don't you _____?以及How about _____?

例句

Can I go to the movies with you?
我可以跟你們去看電影嗎？
Why not?
為什麼不？

會話

A: Why not go camping with us?
=Why don't you go camping with us?
=How about camping with us?
何不跟我們一起去露營？
B: OK.
好啊。
A: Great!
太棒了！

how

【haʊ】

adv. 如何？

當我們要詢問某件事情的方法，方式「如何」，「怎麼」時，句子前要冠上疑問詞how。

例句

How is Mr. Brown?
布朗先生近來如何？
He is fine.
他還不錯。

會話 1

A: How can you make such great cake?
你怎麼做出這麼棒的蛋糕?
B: Practice makes perfect.
熟能生巧啊！

會話 2

A: How do you like your steak?
你的牛排要幾分熟？
B: Well-done, please.
麻煩請全熟。

how much

多少

當我們要詢問多少錢、水、時間等「不可數名詞」的數量有多少時，句子前要冠上疑問詞how much。

例句

How much money does this doll cost?
這個娃娃花了你多少錢?
It costs me 20 dollars.
她花了我二十元。

會話 1

A: How much rent do you pay for the flat?
你這間公寓房租多少?
B: 400 dollars per month.
每個月四百元。

會話 2

A: How much water is there in the container?
水壺裡還有多少水?
B: Not much.
所剩不多了。

how many

多少(人、東西)…

當我們要詢問多少人、東西等「可數名詞複數」的數量有多少時，句子前要冠上疑問詞how many。

例句

How many people are there in your family?
你家有幾個人?

Six people.
六個人。

會話 1

A: How many trees did the gardener plant?
那個園丁種了多少的樹？

B: He planted five trees.
他種了五棵樹。

會話 2

A: How many days do you plan for this trip?
你這趟旅程會待多久?

B: I will stay here for seven days.
我會待在這裡七天。

PART TWO DAILY BASICS

日常最急用

Chapter 2

food

【fud】

n. [C] [U] 食物

健康食物叫作health food，垃圾食物就是junk food。fast food指的是速食，staple food是主食，而comfort food就是吃了會帶來慰藉的食物。

- comfort 【`kʌmfɚt】 n. [U] 舒服，慰藉
- staple 【`stepḷ】 n. [C] 主要食物；訂書針

例句

You can order take-out in a fast-food restaurant.
你可以在速食店點外帶。

Do you want your food "for here" or "to go"?
你要這邊用還是外帶？

會話

A: Hello, can you deliver some food to our company?
嗨，可以請你外送食物到我們公司嗎？

B: Sure. The name of your company, please.
好的。請給我您公司的名字。

diet

【`daɪət】

n. [C] [U] 飲食，食物 vt., vi. 忌食，節食

一般飲食，都可以用diet來統稱，例如排毒餐detox diet。而為減肥而節食，則叫作go on diet；減肥飲食計畫則是diet plan。

■ detox【dɪ`tɑks】adj. 用以解毒的

例句

A balanced diet and exercise can help you keep healthy.
均衡的飲食和運動可以幫助你保持健康。
She is on a diet.
她在節食中。

會話

A: Why don't you have any snacks?
你為什麼不吃零食了呢？
B: Well, I am on a diet because the doctor says that I am too fat.
嗯，我在節食中。因為醫生說我太胖了。

meal

【mil】

n. [C]（一）餐 vt. 進餐

人一天吃三餐，一餐是one meal。用餐時間是mealtime，飛機餐是airplane meal，輕食是light meal。而一份食物我們會說a serving of food或者是one helping of food。

- serving【`sɝvɪŋ】n. [C]（食物一）份
- helping【`hɛlpɪŋ】n. [C]（食物一）份

例句

The Christmas set meals in this restaurant are very special.
這間餐廳的聖誕套餐很特別。
Would you like bread or potatoes with your meal?
你的餐是要配麵包還是馬鈴薯呢？

會話

A: Would you like a drink before your meal?
您用餐前要喝點什麼嗎？
B: I'll have a beer, please.
我要一瓶啤酒。

dinner

【`dɪnɚ】

n. [C] [U] 晚餐，晚宴

正餐(main meal)有三：早餐(breakfast)、午餐(lunch)，以及晚餐(dinner)。晚餐的另一種講法是supper。

- supper 【`sʌpɚ】 n. [C] [U] 晚餐
- lunch 【lʌntʃ】 n. [C] [U] 午餐
- breakfast 【`brɛkfəst】 n. [C] [U] 早餐

例句

When do people have dinner in Hong Kong?
香港人何時吃晚餐？
What are we going to have for supper?
我們晚飯吃什麼？

會話

A: Do you want to eat dinner at my place?
想來我家吃晚餐嗎？
B: My pleasure.
那真是我的榮幸。

vegetable

【`vɛdʒətəb!】

n. [C] [U] 蔬菜；植物

食物有蔬菜(vegetable)，肉類(meat)，跟水果(fruit)。只吃蔬菜水果類的人我們稱做vegetarian。而肉食主義者，英文可以說meat eater，或是meat tooth。最近流行的草食主義者，則叫作herbivore。

- meat 【mit】 n. [U] 肉，肉類
- fruit 【frut】 n. [C] [U] 水果；果實
- vegetarian 【,vɛdʒə`tɛrɪən】 n. [C] 素食者
- herbivore 【`hɝbə,vor】 n. [C] 草食類動物；草食主義者

例句

The Lins grow a lot of vegetables in their yard.
林氏一家人在院子裡種了許多蔬菜。

會話

A: Do you have any vegetarian dishes?
你們有素食餐嗎？

B: Yes, we have noodles with vegetables.
有的，我們有青菜麵。

menu

【`mɛnju】

n. [C] 菜單

菜單上通常會分類成：前菜(appetizer)，主菜(main course)跟甜點(dessert)。有賣酒的餐廳，甚至還會附上酒單(wine list)供顧客選擇。

- appetizer【`æpə,taɪzɚ】n. [C] 前菜，開胃菜
- course【kors】n. [C] 一道菜
- dessert【dɪ`zɝt】n. [C] [U] 甜點
- list【lɪst】n. [C] 列，表，單子

例句

Do you have a menu in Chinese?
你們有中文菜單嗎？

會話

A: May I have a menu, please?
給我菜單好嗎？

B: Sure.
當然。

sides

【saɪdz】

n. pl. 附餐

除了前菜，主菜，甜點之外，有些餐廳還會提供附餐，附餐在英文裡就叫作side dishes或是sides。通常包含有湯(soup)，沙拉(salad)，或是一些小點心(snack)之類的東西。

- soup 【sup】 n. [C] [U] 湯
- salad 【`sæləd】 n. [C] [U] 沙拉
- snack 【snæk】 n. [C] [U] 零食

例句

What would you like for sides?
你要什麼附餐？

會話

A: What sides do you want?
你要什麼附餐？

B: I want some fries, please.
請給我一些薯條。

serve

【sɝv】

vt., vi. 為…服務，上菜

服務生上菜服務，我們都可以用serve來表示。此外，片語wait on也可以用來表示服務。而服務生則是waiter或是waitress。如果服務不錯，可別忘了也服務生小費(tip)喔。

- wait on vt. 服務
- waiter 【`wetɚ】 n. [C] 男服務生
- waitress 【`wetrɪs】 n. [C] 女服務生
- tip 【tɪp】 n. [C] 小費

例 句

The waiter served me a cup of tea.
服務生給我端上一杯茶。

Jill is serving at the table.
吉兒在侍候進餐。

會 話

A: Do you serve alcohol?
這裡有賣酒嗎？

B: No, sorry.
沒有，抱歉啊。

dine

【daɪn】

vt., vi. 用餐

一般吃東西，我們都會用eat這一個動詞，dine除了吃的意思，不過更文雅地表示「用餐」。diner就是用餐者，dining room就是用餐的房間。

- eat 【it】 vt. 吃，食用
- diner 【`daɪnɚ】 n. [C] 用餐者
- dining 【`daɪnɪŋ】 n. [U] 用餐

例句

Jack dined with Linda last night.
傑克昨晚和琳達一起用餐。

Let's dine out tonight.
今晚一起出去吃飯吧。

會話

A: Why not dine out together and go to the movies?
我們何不一起出去吃飯然後去看電影？

B: It sounds great!
這聽起來不錯！

feed

【fid】

vt., vi. **餵，餵食，餵養**

餵別人吃東西，就用feed這一個字。其動詞變化是feed-fed-fed。而I am fed up指的就是「我吃飽了」，也可以說I am full或是I am stuffed。

例句

The babysitter is feeding the baby.
那個保母正在餵小孩。
Do you feed your pet regularly?
你有按時餵你的寵物嗎？

會話

A: What do you feed your cat?
你都為你的貓什麼東西吃？
B: I feed it with canned food.
我都餵它罐頭食品。

hungry

【`hʌŋgrɪ】

adj. 飢餓的，渴望的

挨餓是starve，而口渴的是thirsty。

- starve【stɑrv】vt., vi. 挨餓，餓死
- thirsty【`θɝstɪ】adj. 口渴的，渴望的

例句

The hungry dog watched a piece of bread with its mouth watering.

那隻飢餓的狗流著口水看著一塊麵包。

The beggar was hungry for a nice supper.

那個乞丐渴望有一頓好吃的晚餐。

會話

A: I am so hungry now. I feel like I can eat a horse.

我現在好餓，我覺得我餓到要大吃一頓了。

B: Let's grab a bite now.

我們現在去簡單地吃點東西吧。

reserve

【rɪ`zɝv】

vt. 預約，預訂

要去餐廳用餐，要先預先訂位座位。訂位就是用reserve這一個字。預約就是reservation。當你看到座位上有一張紙上寫著reserved，就表示這個位子有人預訂了。

- reservation 【ˌrɛzə`veʃən】 n. [U] 預約
- reserved 【rɪ`zɝvd】 adj. 預訂的

例句

These seats are reserved for V.I.P.s.
這些座位是為貴賓預留的。

Do you know how to reserve a hotel room in English?
你知道要怎麼預訂英國的旅店嗎？

會話

A: Do you need a reservation?
您要預約嗎？

B: Yes. Please reserve a table for two at eight.
是的。我要預約八點兩個位置。

order

【`ɔrdɚ】

n. [C] 訂單，點菜　vt. 點菜

點菜就是order food。服務生來跟你點餐時，叫作take the order。如果都不知道要點些什麼，可以請服務生推薦(recommend)，或是只接點餐廳的今日特餐(today's special)就好了。

■ recommend【ˌrɛkə`mɛnd】vt. 推薦，介紹

例句

Let me know when you're ready to order.
決定好了再叫我。

Let me repeat your order.
讓我重複一次你點的餐。

會話

A: Could I take your order?
　您要來點什麼？

B: Give me the same order as that.
　我想要一份和那個一樣的。

beverage

【`bɛvərɪdʒ】
n. [C] 飲料

除了beverage，drink也有飲料的意思，不過它在日常用語裡特別指喝酒(drink alcohol)的意思。常見的飲料通常有：酒精類飲料(alcohol)，像是酒(wine)或啤酒(beer)；以及非酒精飲料(soft drinks)像是茶(tea)，咖啡(coffee)，可樂(coke)以及果汁(juice)。

- drink 【drɪŋk】 n. [C] [U] 飲料；vt., vi. 喝
- alcohol 【`ælkə,hɔl】 n. [C] [U] 酒

例句

What kinds of beverages do you want?
你要什麼飲料？
This store does not have a permit to sell alcoholic beverages.
這間店沒有賣酒的許可證。

會話

A: What's your favorite beverage?
你最喜歡喝的飲料是什麼？
B: Coke.
可樂吧！

cook

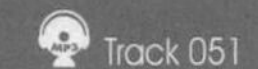

【kʊk】

n. [C] 廚師　vt. 煮飯，做菜

餐廳裡的廚師是cook，主廚則是chef。要注意cooker這一個字指的是廚具，像是pot(鍋子)或是stove(爐子)。而餐具是tableware，像是plate(盤子)，tray(托盤)，spoon(湯匙)或是fork(叉子)。

- chef 【ʃɛf】 n. [C] 主廚
- cook 【kʊk】 n. [C] 廚師
  cooker 【`kʊkɚ】 n. [C] 廚具，烹調器具
- tableware 【`teb!,wɛr】 n. [U] 餐具

例句

Mom always cooks for us.
媽媽總是為我們做飯。
What's your method for cooking this dish?
你煮這道菜的方法是什麼？

會話

A: What does Dave do?
戴夫是做什麼的？
B: He is a cook.
他是一個廚師。

taste

【test】

n. [C] [U] 味道；品味　vt., vi. 嚐…(的味道)；品嘗

食物的味道百百種，像是酸(sour)、甜(sweet)、苦(bitter)、辣(spicy)、鹹(salty)。

- sour 【ˋsaʊr】 adj. 酸的；腐敗的
- salty 【ˋsɔltɪ】 adj. 鹹的
- sweet 【swit】 adj. 甜的
- bitter 【ˋbɪtɚ】 adj. 苦的
- spicy 【ˋspaɪsɪ】 adj. 辛辣的；有香味的

例句

The cake tastes sweet.
這蛋糕嘗起來甜甜的。

會話

A: Does Bill like Mexican food?
比爾喜歡墨西哥食物嗎？

B: Yes. He likes any food with a heavy taste.
是啊，他喜歡任何重口味的食物。

flavor

【`flevɚ】

n. [C] [U] 風味，味道，口味 vt. 給…調味

點甜點時，要巧克力口味或是草莓口味等「口味」，就是用flavor這一個字。另外像是胡椒(pepper)以及鹽(salt)等調味料則是用seasoning這一個字。醬汁則是sauce。

- pepper 【`pɛpɚ】 n. [U] 胡椒粉，黑胡椒
- salt 【sɔlt】 n. [C] [U] 鹽
- seasoning 【`siznɪŋ】 n. [U] 調味品，佐料
- sauce 【sɔs】 n. [C] [U] 醬料

例句

The creamy flavor makes the coffee smooth.
奶油風味使得這咖啡口感滑順。
The chef flavored the salmon with salt.
主廚用鹽巴給鮭魚調味。

會話

A: What flavor ice cream do you like?
你要什麼口味的冰淇淋？
B: Strawberry, please.
請給我草莓的。

restaurant

【`rɛstərənt】

n. [C] 餐廳，飯館

除了一般餐廳之外，café指的是「咖啡廳」，cafeteria指的是「自助餐館」，deli是「熟食店」。而buffet指的是「自助餐」，feast是「大餐」。

- café 【kə`fe】 n. [C] 咖啡廳
- cafeteria 【,kæfə`tɪrɪə】 n. [C] 自助餐館
- deli 【`dɛlɪ】 n. [C] 熟食店
- buffet 【bʌ`fɪt】 n. [C] 自助餐，快餐
- feast 【fist】 n. [C] 盛宴，筵席

例句

There is an Italian restaurant around the corner.
街角有一間義式餐廳。

What restaurant do you recommend?
你推薦哪一間餐廳？

會話

A: Can you tell me if there is any restaurant nearby?
請問這附近有餐廳嗎？

B: What kind of restaurant are you looking for?
你有要找什麼樣的餐廳嗎？

delicious

【dɪ`lɪʃəs】
adj. 好吃的，美味的

食物餐點好吃，我們可以說delicious或是yummy。美食就是delicacy。而難吃的食物，我們會說disgusting或是yuck。

- yummy 【`jʌmɪ】 adj. 美味的
- delicacy 【`dɛləkəsɪ】 n. [C] 美食，佳餚
- disgusting 【dɪs`gʌstɪŋ】 adj. 令人作嘔的
- yuck 【jʌk】 adj. 噁心的，難吃的

例句

This Chinese dish sounds delicious.
這道中國菜聽起來很好吃的樣子。

This croissant tastes delicious.
這個牛角麵包吃起來很好吃。

會話

A: Thank you for the delicious dinner tonight.
謝謝你今晚美味的晚餐。

B: You are welcome. I am too flattered.
別客氣。你真是過獎了。

clothes

Track 054

【kloz】

n. pl. 衣服

cloth是布，而身上一件件的衣服是由很多布所製成，所以我們用clothes來表示衣服。上衣類的衣物(tops)還有：襯衫(shirt)，T恤(T-shirt)，女用襯衫(blouse)等等。

- tops 【tɑps】 n. pl. 上衣
- shirt 【ʃɝt】 n. [C] 襯衫
- T-shirt 【`tiˏʃɝt】 n. [C] T恤
- blouse 【blaʊz】 n. [C] 女用襯衫

例句

Clothes make the man.
人要衣裝。
Your clothes don't match.
你的衣服看起來不搭配。

會話

A: Where are you going?
　你要去哪兒？
B: I am going to shop for some clothes and shoes.
　我要去買些衣服跟鞋子。

wear

【wɛr】

vt. 穿，戴

穿衣服在英文裡有多種講法，一般來說，wear是最通用的，而put on強調「穿起來」這個動作，dress up則有「盛裝打扮」的意味。而在服飾店裡「試穿」則是try on。「脫下衣服」則是take off。wear的動詞三態變化為wear-wore-worn。

- put on v. phr. 穿上，戴上
- dress up v. phr. 裝扮
- try on v. phr. 試穿
- take off v. phr. 脫掉(衣服)

例句

That student wears a pair of glasses.
那個學生戴了一副眼鏡。

會話

A: What size do you wear?
你穿幾號？

B: Six, please.
請給我六號。

costume

【`kastjum】

n. [C] [U] 服裝，裝束

服裝也有很多講法，像是dress指的是「洋裝」，suit通常指男生的「西裝」，而gown指的會是「長禮服」。casual wear則是「便服」。sportswear是「運動服」。

- dress 【drɛs】 n. [C] 禮服，連衣裙
- suit 【sut】 n. [C] (一套)衣服
- gown 【gaʊn】 n. [C] 長禮服，長袍
- casual 【`kæʒʊəl】 adj. 隨便的，不經心的
- wear 【wɛr】 n. [C] 衣服，服飾

例句

Children wear special costumes for Halloween.
孩子為了萬聖節穿上特別的服裝。

會話

A: Stacy wore a fancy costume to the party last night.
史黛西昨晚穿了一件花俏的服裝參加宴會。

B: Wow, it sounds funny.
哇，這聽起來真好笑。

size

【saɪz】

n. [C] [U] 尺寸

買衣服首先要注意它尺寸合不合適。吊牌上的L指的是large(大)，M是medium(中)，S是small(小)。而像是XL或是XS的X指的是extra。

- large 【lɑrdʒ】 adj. 大的
- medium 【`midɪəm】 adj. 中間的，中等的
- small 【smɔl】 adj. 小的
- extra 【`ɛkstrə】 adj., adv. 額外的

例句

Do you want to try this same dress in a different size?
你要試穿這款禮服別的尺寸嗎？
What size Coke do you want?
你可樂要多大杯？

會話

A: What's your shoe size, please?
請問您鞋子穿幾號的？
B: Do you have a size five?
你們有五號鞋嗎？

suit

【sut】

vt. 與…相配，與…相稱

除了尺寸上的合適之外，外觀上的合適，好不好看也是挑選衣服的重點。合適我們可以說appropriate，而合身是fit。跟你很配很搭是suit，match，或是go with you。好看則是good-looking。

- appropriate 【ə`proprɪ,et】 adj. 適當的，恰當的
- fit 【fɪt】 vt. 合…身，與…相稱
- go with vt. 與…相配
- good-looking 【`gʊd`lʊkɪŋ】 adj. 好看的

例句

This outfit suits you very well.
這件套裝非常合適你。

會話

A: My mother bought this pair of jeans for me the other day.
前些天我媽幫我買了這條牛仔褲。

B: But they don't really fit you well.
但是它不太適合你喔。

color

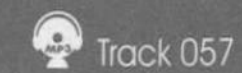

【`kʌlɚ】

n. [C] [U] 顏色，色彩　vt., vi. 染色，上色

挑選服飾，顏色也是很多人考量的因素。常見的顏色有：紅(red)、橙(orange)、黃(yellow)、綠(green)、藍(blue)、靛(indigo)、紫(purple)。大多數人會挑選的黑(black)、白(white)、灰(grey)，是不屬於色彩的範圍喔。

- black 【blæk】 adj., n. [U] 黑色的；黑色
- white 【hwaɪt】 adj., n. [U] 白色的；白色
- grey 【gre】 adj., n. [U] 灰色的；灰色

例句

Kelly's favorite color is pink.
凱莉最喜歡的顏色是粉紅色。

Sam colored the picture green.
山姆將畫塗上綠色。

會話

A: What color shirt goes with brown pants?
什麼顏色的襯衫可以搭咖啡褲子？

B: I would say baby blue.
我會說淺藍色。

bright

【braɪt】

adj. 明亮的，鮮明的

顏色有明暗的色調之分，像是亮黃色是bright yellow，而深棕色是dark brown。淺藍色是light blue。

- dark【dɑrk】adj. 深(色)的，暗的
- light【laɪt】adj. 淺(色)的

例句

Have you seen a bright red car passing by?
你有看到一台輛紅色的車經過嗎？
The sunlight is bright.
陽光很明亮。

會話

A: Georgia dyed her hair bright orange.
喬治亞把她的頭髮染成亮橘色的。
B: Really!
真的嗎！

trend

【trɛnd】

n. [C] 趨勢，時尚

很多人挑選衣服，也會在乎流不流行的問題。trend跟fashion都可以表是潮流時尚的意思。當我們要稱讚某人穿得很潮，我們可以說：You are in，或是You are trendy。

- fashion 【`fæʃən】 n. [C] [U] 流行，時尚，風氣
- in 【ɪn】 adj. 流行的，時髦的
- trendy 【`trɛndɪ】 adj. 流行的，時髦的

例句

Learning Mandarin has become a worldwide trend.
學華文已經成為國際的趨勢。

The real fashionable people are not those who follow the trends, but those who lead the trend.
真正時尚的人不是那些跟流行的人，而是那些引導潮流的人。

會話

A: Can you recommend some clothes for me?
你可以跟我推薦一些衣服嗎？

B: How about these shirts? The latest trend is towards smart casual.
這些襯衫如何？最新的潮流是體面的休閒穿著。

funny

【`fʌnɪ】
adj.滑稽可笑的；古怪的

有些人混搭的不好，就不會看起來潮或是酷(cool)，而是滑稽了。看起來奇怪，可笑還有strange跟ridiculous可用。

- cool 【kul】 adj. 涼爽的，酷的
- ridiculous 【rɪ`dɪkjələs】 adj. 可笑的，荒謬的

例句

The clown looked funny.
這個小丑看起來很滑稽。
There are many funny games on the Internet.
網路上有許多奇怪的遊戲。

會話

A: Guess what? Alice wears a purple shirt to go with her green skirt.
你猜怎麼了，愛麗絲穿一件紫襯衫配上一條綠裙子。
B: She looks so funny.
她看起來真滑稽。

pair

【pɛr】

n. [C] 一對，一雙

很多成雙成對的東西，像是手套(glove)，褲子(trousers或是pants)，鞋子(shoes)，眼鏡(glasses)之類的東西，在英文裡我們都會用a pair of來表示他們的數量。

- glove 【glʌv】 n. [C] 手套
- trouser 【\`traʊzɚ】 n. [C] 褲子
- pants 【pænts】 n. pl. 褲子
- shoe 【ʃu】 n. [C] 鞋子
- glasses 【\`glæsɪz】 n. pl. 眼鏡

例句

I am looking for a pair of boots.
我在找一雙靴子。

會話

A: I am looking for a pair of shoes to go with my blue dress.
我在找一雙能配我藍洋裝的鞋。

B: How about this pair?
這一雙好嗎？

accessory

【æk`sɛsərɪ】

n. [C] 附件，裝飾品

服飾搭配，小飾品扮演著畫龍點睛的功效。像是項鍊(necklace)、耳環(earning)、戒指(ring)、手鍊(bracelet)、腰帶(belt)、包包(bag)之類的東西都是屬於附件小飾品。

necklace 【`nɛklɪs】 n. [C] 項鍊
earring 【`ɝ͵rɪŋ】 n. [C] 耳環
ring 【rɪŋ】 n. [C] 戒指
bracelet 【`breslɪt】 n. [C] 手鍊，手環
belt 【bɛlt】 n. [C] 皮帶
bag 【bæg】 n. [C] 包包，袋子

例句

Claire runs a shop of accessories and jewelry for young women.
克萊兒經營一間輕熟女飾品珠寶店。

會話

A: Can you please help me pick out some accessories?
可以請你幫我挑一些配件嗎？

B: Sure.
好啊。

cosmetics

【kaz`mɛtɪks】

n. [C] [U] 化妝品，美容品

近年來，化妝也漸漸併入整體搭配的一部分。化妝品除了cosmetics之外，我們還可以說make-up。常見的化妝品有唇膏(lip stick)、粉底(foundation)、腮紅(blusher)、眼影(eye shadow)以及香水(perfume)等等。

- make-up 【`mek,ʌp】 n. [C] [U] 化妝品
- lipstick 【`lɪp,stɪk】 n. [C] [U] 口紅
- foundation 【faʊn`deʃən】 n. [C] [U] 粉底
- blush 【blʌʃ】 n. [C] [U] 腮紅
- eye shadow n. [C] [U] 眼影
- perfume 【pɚ`fjum】 n. [C] [U] 香水

例句

There is a full range of cosmetics in this store.
這一間店有全系列的化妝品。

會話

A: I want to buy some cosmetics. Can you wait for me?
我想要買些化妝品。你可以等我嗎？

B: OK.
好吧。

expensive

【ɪk`spɛnsɪv】

adj. 昂貴的

便宜的是cheap，而物美價廉的是inexpensive，價錢合理的是reasonable。

- cheap 【tʃip】 adj. 便宜的，低廉的
- inexpensive 【,ɪnɪk`spɛnsɪv】 adj. 物美價廉的，價錢不高的
- reasonable 【`riznəb!】 adj. (價錢)合理的，公道的

例句

Lisa cannot afford that expensive dress.
麗莎買不起那件昂貴的洋裝。

That leather jacket is very expensive.
那件皮衣非常昂貴。

會話

A: This brand-name bag cost me 60,000 dollars.
這個名牌包花了我六萬元。

B: That's really expensive.
那真的很貴。

slim

【slɪm】

adj. 苗條的，微薄的

穿衣服也要看身材(figure)。胖的是fat，纖瘦的還有slender，中等身材是medium，而嬌小的是petite。

- figure 【`fɪgjɚ】 n. [C] 身材，體型
- slender 【`slɛndɚ】 adj. 纖瘦的
- petite 【pə`tit】 adj. 嬌小的

例句

Exercising can help you lose weight and keep slim.
運動可以幫你減重並保持體態纖細。

The old man's chances for recovery were very slim.
那個老先生康復的機率很渺茫。

會話

A: You look very slim in that dress.
你穿那件洋裝看起來真瘦。

B: Thank you.
謝謝你。

house

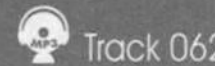

【haʊs】

n. [C] 房子，住宅

常言道，家不只是房子(A home is more than a house.)，家跟房子，我們在英文裡用的字也不同。除了house跟home，household指的是「家庭」或是「戶」的意思。而一般建築物則是building。

- home 【hom】 n. [C] [U] 住家，家庭
- household 【`haʊs,hold】 n. [C] 家庭，戶
- building 【`bɪldɪŋ】 n. [C] [U] 建築物；建築

例句

Frank cannot afford a house in the city.
法蘭克買不起城裡的房子。

會話

A: Where is Wendy's new house?
溫蒂的新房子在哪兒？

B: It's in town.
它就在城裡。

room

【rum】

n. [C] [U] 房間，室；空間

room service指的是客房服務，roommate是室友。living room是客廳，study room是書房，而臥室是bed room。

- mate 【met】 n. [C] 同伴，夥伴
- living 【`lɪvɪŋ】 n. [U] 生活
- study 【`stʌdɪ】 n. [U] 學習，研究

例句

Maria greeted her guests in the living room.
瑪麗亞在客廳接待她的客人。
This hotel is famous for its room service.
這間旅店以它的客房服務聞名。

會話

A: Where did you put your bag?
你把包包放在哪兒？
B: I put it in my bedroom.
我把它放在我的臥房了。

kitchen

【`kɪtʃɪn】

n. [C] 廚房

房子裡少不了做菜的地方，廚房是kitchen，而用餐的地方就叫作dining room。

例句

Sue got all the kitchen appliances she needed in the shopping mall.
蘇在購物中心購齊她所需的廚房用品。

There is a leak in the kitchen sink.
廚房水槽漏水。

會話

A: Where is Nina?
妮娜在哪裡？

B: She is cleaning the kitchen.
她在打掃廚房。

bathroom

【`bæθ,rum】

n. [C] 浴室

bath是沐浴、洗澡，所以bathtub指的是浴缸，bath towel是浴巾，bath salt是浴鹽，bathrobe是澡袍。而浴室地板溼溼滑滑，記得一定要穿slippers(拖鞋)，以確保安全喔。

- tub 【tʌb】 n. [C] 盆子，浴缸
- towel 【`taʊəl】 n. [C] 毛巾
- robe 【rob】 n. [C] 袍子
- slipper 【`slɪpɚ】 n. [C] 拖鞋

例句

Winnie likes to take a hot bath in the bathroom in winter.
溫妮喜歡在冬天裡在浴室泡澡。

Iris likes to decorate her bathroom.
艾瑞絲喜歡裝飾她的浴室。

會話

A: Excuse me, is there a bathroom around here?
不好意思，這附近有廁所嗎？

B: There's a public toilet just outside and to your right.
出去右手邊有一間公廁。

toilet

【`tɔɪlɪt】

n. [C] 廁所；馬桶

廁所還有許多其他的講法，像是lavatory(盥洗室)，restroom(休息室)，lady's room(女廁)，man's room(男廁)，或是英式的W.C.(water closet)。

- lavatory 【`lævə,torɪ】 n. [C] 盥洗室，洗手間
- restroom n. [C] 休息室，洗手間
- closet 【`klɑzɪt】 n. [C] 櫥櫃

例句

The toilet is occupied at the moment.
現在廁所有人。

The toilet won't flush.
這馬桶無法沖水。

會話

A: May I use your toilet, please?
我可以跟你借廁所嗎？

B: Yes. It's down the corridor.
可以啊，它在走廊的盡頭。

shower

【`ʃaʊɚ】

n. [C] 淋浴，淋浴間 vt., vi. 淋浴

淋浴沖澡，是take a shower，清洗是wash，而泡澡是take a bath。冬天去泡的暖呼呼溫泉，則是hot spring。

- wash 【wɑʃ】 vt. 清洗
- spring 【sprɪŋ】 n. [U] 泉水

例句

Many westerners usually take a shower in the morning.
許多西方人通常在早上洗澡。

You can purchase various shower gels in this department store.
你可以在這間百貨公司買到各式各樣的沐浴乳。

會話

A: Please take a shower before you enter the swimming pool.
進入游泳池前請先淋浴。

B: No problem.
沒問題。

furniture

【`fɝnɪtʃɚ】
n. [U] 傢俱

傢俱是不可數名詞，所以我們會說一組傢俱：a set of furniture。傢俱有桌子(table)，書桌(desk)，椅子(chair)，沙發(sofa)，或是櫃子(shelf)之類的。

- set 【sɛt】 n. [C] (一)組，套
- table【`teb!】 n. [C] 桌子，餐桌
- desk 【dɛsk】 n. [C] 桌子，書桌
- chair 【tʃɛr】 n. [C] 椅子
- sofa 【`sofə】 n. [C] 沙發椅
- shelf 【ʃɛlf】 n. [C] 櫃子，書櫃

例句

Christine majors in furniture design.
克莉斯汀主修家具設計。

會話

A: How may I help you, sir?
我能為您效勞嗎？
B: I am looking for a new furniture set for my study.
我在為我的書房找一組新家具。

appliance

【ə`plaɪəns】

n. [C] 用具；設備

家電用品是household appliances，包含有電視(television)，冰箱(refrigerator)，洗衣機(washing machine)，吹風機(hair dryer)或是洗碗機(dish washer)等。

- television 【`tɛlə,vɪʒən】 n. [C] 電視(簡稱TV)
- refrigerator 【rɪ`frɪdʒə,retɚ】 n. [C] 電冰箱
- machine 【mə`ʃin】 n. [C] 機器
- dryer 【`draɪɚ】 n. [C] 烘乾機，吹風機

例句

There is an electric appliance store outside of town.
鎮外有一間電器行。

The living room is equipped with modern household appliances.
這間客廳設有現代的家電用品。

會話

A: Where can I get some office appliances?
我可以去哪拿些辦公用品？

B: You can have some from the general affairs office.
你可以到總務部門去拿。

hotel

【ho`tɛl】

n. [C] 旅館，旅社

旅行之中的家，就是旅店了。除了hotel，還有汽車旅館(motel)，青年旅舍(hostel)，小客棧(tavern或是inn)跟民宿(B&B)。

- motel 【mo`tɛl】 n. [C] 汽車旅館
- hostel 【`hɑst!】 n. [C] 青年旅舍
- tavern 【`tævɚn】 n. [C] 小客棧
- inn 【ɪn】 n. [C] 小客棧
- B&B = bed and breakfast 民宿

例句

It is easy to book a hotel room online.
在網路上訂飯店房間很容易。
Lucy made a reservation for a hotel room over the phone.
露西透過電話訂了一個飯店房間。

會話

A: Do you prefer staying in a hotel or staying in a B&B?
你喜歡住旅店還是民宿？
B: I prefer staying in a B&B.
我比較喜歡住在民宿裡。

live

【lɪv】

vi. 居住，生活

住在房子裡，我們除了live可以用之外，同義字還有dwell，reside以及及物動詞inhabit。而居民則叫作resident或inhabitant。

- dwell 【dwɛl】 vi. 居住
- reside 【rɪ`zaɪd】 vi. 居住
- inhabit 【ɪn`hæbɪt】 vt. 居住
- resident 【`rɛzədənt】 n. [C] 居民
- inhabitant 【ɪn`hæbətənt】 n. [C] 居民

例句

Sandy has lived here for more than ten years.
珊蒂住在這裡已經超過十年了。

The refugees lived a life of misery.
難民過著悲慘的生活。

會話

A: Where do you live?
你住在哪裡？

B: I live in Taichung.
我住在台中。

apartment

【ə`partmənt】

n. [C] 公寓

如果沒有自己的房子，大多數的人就會去租公寓(或是flat)。房東是landlord或是landlady，而房客就是tenant。室友是roommate。

- flat 【flæt】 n. [C] 公寓
- landlord 【`lænd,lɔrd】 n. [C] 男房東
- landlady 【`lænd,ledɪ】 n. [C] 女房東
- tenant 【`tɛnənt】 n. [C] 房客
- roommate 【`rum,met】 n. [C] 室友

例句

Many people rent apartments in big cities.
許多人在大城市裡租公寓。

會話

A: Hello, may I help you?
您好，你需要些什麼呢？

B: I would like to rent an apartment.
我想要租一間公寓。

clean

【klin】

vt., vi. 清理，打掃 adj. 乾淨的

住在房子裡，過一陣子就要好好清理打掃，讓自己有一個舒適的居住環境。打掃工具有掃把(broom)、拖把(mop)、吸塵器(vacuum cleaner)等。

- broom 【brum】 n. [C] 掃把
- mop 【mɑp】 n. [C] 拖把
- vacuum 【`vækjʊəm】 n. [C] 真空
- cleaner 【`klinɚ】 n. [C] 清潔劑

例句

The maid is cleaning the house.
那個女僕正在清理房子。

The water in the stream is very clean.
溪流裡的水很乾淨。

會話

A: It's time to clean you room. It's messy!
該是你打掃房間的時候了。真亂！

B: OK, Mom.
好吧，媽媽。

dirty

【`dɝtɪ】

vt., vi. 弄髒；變髒　adj. 骯髒的

房子久沒整理就會變髒，混亂是mess，零亂不堪的樣子是messy，整齊的樣子是tidy。

- mess 【mɛs】 n. [U] [C] 混亂，凌亂
- messy 【`mɛsɪ】 adj. 混亂的，骯髒的
- tidy 【`taɪdɪ】 adj. 整齊的

例句

The abandoned house is very dirty.
這間廢棄屋十分骯髒。
These children dirtied the floor with paints.
這些小孩用顏料把地板弄髒了。

會話

A: God, your clothes are so dirty.
天哪，你的衣服真髒。
B: I will have them washed.
我要洗衣服了。

junk

【dʒʌŋk】

n. [U] 垃圾，廢物

垃圾的其他說法還有garbage、rubbish跟trash。垃圾桶則是trash can。junk mail是垃圾郵件，垃圾食物是junk food。

- garbage 【`gɑrbɪdʒ】 n. [U] 垃圾，廢物
- rubbish 【`rʌbɪʃ】 n. [U] 垃圾，廢物
- trash 【træʃ】 n. [U] 垃圾，廢物

例句

William threw away all the junk in his room.
威廉把他房裡的垃圾都丟了。

Chips and fried chicken are two kinds of junk food.
洋芋片跟炸雞是兩種垃圾食物。

會話

A: Can you help me dump the garbage?
你可以當我倒垃圾嗎？

B: No problem.
沒問題。

fix

【fɪks】

vt. 修理

門(door)，窗(window)，傢俱，家電用品用久了就要修理，除了fix，我們還可以用repair。

- door 【dor】 n. [C] 門
- window 【`wɪndo】 n. [C] 窗
- repair 【rɪ`pɛr】 vt. 修理

例句

The plumber tried to fix the sink.
水電工試著把水槽修好。

My brother had his computer fixed.
我哥把他的電腦拿去修。

會話

A: Can you fix the copier?
你能修理這台影印機嗎？

B: Yes.
可以。

garden

【`gardən】
n. [C] 花園

大一點的房子，就會有前庭(front yard)、後院(back yard)。在大一些的房子，甚至會有需要園丁(gardener)照顧的花園以及氣派的大門(gate)。

- yard 【jard】 n. [C] 院子
- gardener 【`gardənɚ】 n. [C] 園丁
- gate 【get】 n. [C] 大門

例句

Helen held a garden party this weekend.
海倫這周末辦了場花園派對。
There are many roses in the Hyde's Garden.
海德公園裡有許多玫瑰。

會話

A: There is a small garden in my house.
我家有一個小花園。
B: Wow, that's wonderful.
哇，那真是太棒了。

transportation

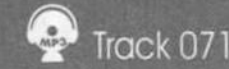

【ˌtrænspɚˋteʃən】

n. [U] 交通，運輸

交通方式就叫作a means of transportation。大家每日通勤(commute)的方式百百種，像是搭捷運(MRT)，公車(bus)，或是計程車(taxi)，都是a means of transportation。

- means 【minz】 n. [C] 方式
- MRT= mass rapid transit 大眾快速運輸
- commute【kəˋmjut】 vi. 通勤

例句

Buses and the MRT are public transportation.
公車跟捷運是公眾交通工具。

The city owns its mass transportation system.
這個城市有自己的大眾運輸系統。

會話

A: Do you have transportation to the airport?
你們有到機場的交通工具嗎？

B: Yes, you can take the shuttle bus.
有的，你可以搭乘接駁車。

walk

【wɔk】

vt., vi. 走路，行走 n. [C] 走路，行走

最普遍跟最天然的交通方式應該就是行走了吧！on feet 也有表示行走的意思。而散步、漫遊，我們還可以用wander，roam或是stroll這些字來表示。

- foot 【fʊt】 n. [C] 腳 複數型是feet
- wander 【`wandɚ】 vi. 流浪，漫遊
- roam 【rom】 vi. 漫遊，散步
- stroll 【strol】 vi. 漫遊，散步

例句

Matt helps his sister walk her dog.
麥特幫他姊姊遛狗。

Diane likes to take a walk after dinner.
戴安喜歡在晚飯後散步。

會話

A: How do you commute?
你的通勤方式是什麼？

B: I walk to the office.
我走路上班。

turn

【tɝn】

n. [C] 轉角，轉彎處 vt., vi. 轉向，轉彎；轉換

路邊街角是corner。右轉是turn right，而左轉是turn left。

- corner 【`kɔrnɚ】 n. [C] 轉角
- right 【raɪt】 adj., adv. 右邊的
- left 【lɛft】 adj., adv. 左邊的

例句

The car made a sharp turn.
這輛車急轉彎。
Please turn off the light.
請關燈。

會話

A: Where can I find stationery?
我在哪裡可以找到文具？
B: Walk along aisle three to the end, turn left and you will see it.
三號走道直走到底，左轉你就會看到了。

route

【rut】

n. [C] 路線，途徑

公車的行徑路線，或是行車紀錄器所規劃的路線，在英文裡我們都可以用route這個字表示。地圖是map，而journey指的行程，而travel指的是行進跟旅行。

- map 【mæp】 n. [C] 地圖
- journey 【`dʒɝnɪ】 n. [C] 行程；旅程
- travel 【`træv!】 vt., vi. 旅行

例句

The climbers tried to find a new route to the top of the mountain.
登山者試著找出一條到山頂的新路。
Tom is reading the route map, figuring out which bus he should take.
湯姆讀著路線圖，想知道他應該搭哪一台公車。

會話

A: I think we are lost. Do you know the route?
我想我們迷路了。你知道路怎麼走嗎？
B: Well, here is the map.
嗯，這裡有地圖。

direction

【də`rɛkʃən】

n. [C] [U] 方向

方位，方向我們會用direction表示，指南針是compass。東邊是east，西邊是west，南邊是south，而北邊是north。

■ compass【`kʌmpəs】 n. [C] 指南針

例句

Which direction is it to the central station?
往火車站的方向是哪？
That foreigner got bad directions and got lost in town.
那個外國人方向感不好，並在鎮裡迷路了。

會話

A: Where is the theater?
請問戲院在哪兒？
B: I am afraid that you are walking in the opposite direction.
恐怕你走反方向了。

move

【muv】

vt., vi. 移動，搬動，行進

前移是move forward，往後移是move backward。move on跟move along都是繼續向前移動的意思。

- forward 【`fɔrwɚd】 adv. 向前地
- backward 【`bækwɚd】 adv. 向後地

例句

The Lins will be moving out on Tuesday.
林家人星期二會搬出去。

Move out of my way!
讓開！

會話

A: John, help me move the chairs.
約翰，幫忙搬一下椅子。

B: OK.
好的。

road

【rod】

n. [C] 道路，馬路

way也有路的意思，而path也是道路的意思，但是比較偏向小徑。boulevard則是大道，大馬路的意思。

- way 【we】 n. [C] 道路
- path 【pæθ】 n. [C] 小徑，道路
- boulevard 【`bulə,vard】 n. [C] 大道，大馬路

例句

The road divides here.
這條路在這裡分岔。

Peter hopes to go on a road trip.
彼得想來趟公路之旅。

會話

A: Where is the museum?
博物館在哪裡？

B: Go straight down this road and turn right at the second intersection.
這條路直走，然後在第二個紅綠燈右轉。

street

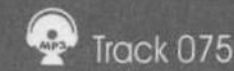

【strit】

n. [C] 巷子

除了道路之外，我們還有街道，以及巷弄(alley)與小路(lane)。此外，在路牌上常見的avenue指的是大街。

- alley 【`ælɪ】 n. [C] 小巷，小弄
- lane 【len】 n. [C] 小巷，小路
- avenue 【`ævə,nju】 n. [C] 大街

例句

Wall Street is the financial center of America.
華爾街是美國的金融中心。
No spitting on the street.
街上禁止吐痰。

會話

A: Excuse me. Where is this hotel?
不好意思，請問一下這間飯店在那裡？
B: Just across the street.
就在對街。

station

【`steʃən】

n. [C] 車站

終點站是terminal station，火車站是train station。stop當名詞用，也有車站的意思，像是bus stop是公車站。抵達車站我們會說reach the station。

- terminal 【`tɝmən!】 adj. 末期的，終點的
- stop 【stɑp】 n. [C] 站牌
- reach 【ritʃ】 vt. 抵達，到達

例句

The terminal station of this train is Kaoshiung.
這輛火車的終點站是高雄。
Gina got off at Walnut Station.
吉娜在胡桃街下車。

會話

A: Could you tell me where the train station is?
你可以告訴我火車站在哪兒？
B: There's a bus you can take to get to the station.
那裡的公車有到火車站。

traffic

【`træfɪk】
n. [U] 交通

traffic lights是紅綠燈，traffic island是安全島，traffic jam是交通堵塞。heavy traffic指的也是在尖峰時刻(rush hour)時的交通擁擠。

- island 【`aɪlənd】 n. [C] 島嶼
- jam 【dʒæm】 n. [C] [U] 擁擠，堵塞；果醬
- rush 【rʌʃ】 n. [U] 忙碌，繁忙

例句

Cars are stuck in a traffic jam in rush hour.
在尖峰時刻車輛被困在車陣當中。
The traffic in a big city is heavy all the time.
大城市的交通總是十分擁塞。

會話

A: Sorry for being late. The traffic in Taipei this morning is really heavy.
抱歉遲到了，今天早上台北的交通真塞。
B: Well, it's OK.
嗯，沒關係。

vehicle

【`viɪk!】

n. [C] **車輛，載具**

路上的車輛我們都可以泛稱vehicle。細分起來，我們會有腳踏車(bicycle)，機車(motorcycle)，汽車(car)，公車(bus)。

- bicycle 【`baɪsɪk!】 n. [C] 腳踏車(可簡稱bike)
- motorcycle 【`motɚ,saɪk!】 n. [C] 機車
- car 【kɑr】 n. [C] 汽車
- bus 【bʌs】 n. [C] 公車

例句

Henry just bought a sport utility vehicle.
亨利剛買了輛運動休旅車。

The importance of vehicle safety cannot be overemphasized.
汽車安全十分重要。

會話

A: I am looking for a new car. What do you recommend?
我在找輛新車。你推薦哪一台？

B: How about this one? It is a very energy-efficient vehicle.
這台如何？這是一台非常節能的車。

ride

【raɪd】

vt., vi. 騎乘　n. [C] 騎乘，乘坐

騎腳踏車，騎馬，騎機車，我們都會用ride這一個動詞。而開車則會用drive，駕駛的意思。但是如果是搭乘大眾交通工具，我們就會用take，像是take a train(搭火車)或是take a taxi(搭計程車)。

- drive【draɪv】vt., vi. 駕駛
- train【tren】n. [C] 火車
- taxi【`tæksɪ】n. [C] 計程車

例句

Alice rides home on her bicycle every day.
愛麗絲每天騎腳踏車回家。

How long is the bus ride?
這趟公車要做多久？

會話

A: Do you want to go to the amusement park with us?
你要跟我們一起去遊樂園嗎？

B: No, thanks. I am too old to ride on the roller coaster.
不用了，謝謝。我太老不敢玩雲霄飛車了。

driver

【`draɪvɚ】

n. [C] 駕駛

汽車駕駛是driver，機車，或是腳踏車騎士我們稱呼rider。cyclist 也可以用來表示腳踏車騎士，去騎腳踏車是go cycling。

- rider 【`raɪdɚ】 n. [C] 騎乘者，騎士
- cyclist 【`saɪk!ɪst】 n. [C] 腳踏車騎士
- cycle 【`saɪk!】 vt. 循環，騎腳踏車

例句

George works as a taxi driver.
喬治是一名計程車駕駛。

Vivian finally got a driver's license.
薇薇安終於拿到駕照了。

會話

A: What does Ben do?
班是做什麼的？

B: He is a bus driver.
他是公車司機。

accident

【`æksədənt】

n. [C] 意外；事故

car accident是車禍的意思，我們也可以說car crash。

■ crash【kræʃ】n. [C] 相撞(事故)

例句

The car accident was really dreadful and many people were killed.

那場車禍真的很恐怖，而且很多人喪生於此。

The encounter seemed to have happened by accident.

這場邂逅似乎是偶然發生的。

會話

A: Why is the train delayed?

為什麼火車誤點？

B: There might have been a railway accident.

稍早可能有鐵道事故吧。

guide

【gaɪd】

vt. 引導，為…引路　n. [C] 引導者，指南

guide當名詞，可以指導遊(tour guide)，也可以指旅行指南書(guidebook)。

例句

The waiter guided them to the reserved table.
服務生引導他們到預定的座位。
Charles works as a tour guide in China.
查理在中國當導遊。

會話

A: Do you have the book "London Shopping Street Guidc"?
你們有「倫敦街道購物導覽」這本書嗎？
B: Yes. It's in aisle five.
有的，在第五個走道。

reach

【ritʃ】 vt., vi. 抵達；達到

n. [C] [U] (手、腳、交通工具、能力)可及之範圍

reach for是伸手去拿(東西)，within reach是觸手可及，out of reach是只拿不到的範圍。

例句

When will we reach the destination?
我們什麼時候抵達終點？

Taiwan is a small island where everything is within reach.
台灣是一個小島，任何事物都觸手可及。

會話

A: What time does the train reach Paris?
這火車何時會抵達巴黎？

B: You should be there at 1:30.
你應該1點半會到。

study

【`stʌdɪ】

vt., vi. 學，學習；研究 n. [C] [U] 學習；研究

講到教育，先想到的就是學習，除了study，英文裡還有learn也可以表示學習。而學生就是student。

- learn 【lɝn】 vt. 學習
- student 【`stjudnt】 n. [C] 學生

例句

In this lesson, we'll study the behavior of fish.
在這堂課哩，我們將要學習魚類的行為。

That postgraduate wrote a study of Ernest Hemingway.
那名研究生寫了一篇關於海明威的研究。

會話

A: Does Kathy plan to study abroad?
凱西計畫要出國念書嗎？

B: Yes, and she's decided to study fashion design in France.
對啊，而且她已經決定要在法國學習時尚設計。

acquire

【ə`kwaɪr】

vt. 學習，學會

真的學會一個技能或語言，我們會用acquire這一個動詞。pick up表示不經意學會某個語言，而master則表示精通。

- pick up v. phr. (不經意)學會
- master【`mæstɚ】vt. 精通

例句

Jimmy finally acquired a large vocabulary with the assistance of his teacher.
在老師的協助之下，吉米終於學會了很多字彙。

Students not only have to acquire knowledge in school but also develop the ability to think independently.
學生不只是要在學校習得知識，而且還要發展獨立思考的能力。

會話

A: I want to acquire Korean quickly.
我想要趕快學會韓文。

B: Then, you have to study very hard.
那麼，你要非常努力學。

teach

【titʃ】

vt. 教，教會…

teacher是老師。而instruct是指導，instructor是指導者。mentor是導師的意思。要注意teach的動詞變化為teach-taught-taught。

- instruct 【ɪn`strʌkt】 vt. 指導
- instructor 【`ɪnstə,tjutɚ】 n. [C] 指導者，老師
- mentor 【`mɛntɚ】 n. [C] 導師

例句

The coach has taught children swimming for ten years.
這個教練已經教小孩子游泳十年了。

That car accident taught Chloe a lesson.
那場車禍給了克勞伊一個教訓。

會話

A: I like skating very much, but is it easy to learn?
我很喜歡溜冰，但是那容易學嗎？

B: Yes, it is. I can teach you if you like.
容易啊。如果你要的話，我可以教你。

educate

【`ɛdʒə,ket】
vt. 教育，教化

教育是education，教育部是Ministry of Education，教育家是educator。

- education 【,ɛdʒʊ`keʃən】 n. [U] 教育
- ministry 【`mɪnɪstrɪ】 n. [C] 部
- educator 【`ɛdʒʊ,ketɚ】 n. [C] 教育家，教育人員

例句

It takes patience and love to educate children.
教育小孩需要耐心跟愛心。
Many parents do not know how to properly educate their children.
許多家長不知道如何適當地教育他們的孩子。

會話

A: What is your favorite TV show?
你最喜歡的電視節目是什麼？
B: Animal Planet, because it educates the audience about things in the animal world.
「動物星球」。因為它教育觀眾關於動物世界的事情。

classroom

【`klæs,rʊm】

n. [C] 教室

同學是classmate，圖書館是library，保健中心是health center，而實驗室是laboratory，校園是campus。

- classmate 【`klæs,met】 n. [C] 同學
- library 【`laɪ,brɛrɪ】 n. [C] 圖書館
- laboratory 【`læbrə,torɪ】 n. [C] 實驗室(=lab)
- campus 【`kæmpəs】 n. [U] 校園

例句

The students quietly took an exam in a classroom.
學生們在教室裡安靜地考試。

It is not easy for a new teacher to manage his or her classroom properly.
對一位新老師來說適當地管理教室是不容易的。

會話

A: Joshua, will you help us with classroom decorations?
喬許華，你可以幫我們教室佈置嗎？

B: Of course, I would love to.
當然啊，我很樂意。

school

【skul】

n. [C] 學校

elementary school是小學，junior high school是國中，高中是senior high school，職業學校是vocational school，補習班則是cram school。

- elementary 【ˌɛlə`mɛntərɪ】 adj. 基礎的
- junior 【`dʒunjɚ】 adj. 資淺的
- senior 【`sinjɚ】 adj. 資深的
- vocational 【vo`keʃən!】 adj. 職業的
- cram 【kræm】 vt. 擠，塞

例句

Which public school do you go to?
你就讀你一所公立學校？

會話

A: How was your day at school today?
你今天在學校過的如何？

B: It was a disaster. I was called on in English class and I could not understand the question the teacher asked.
今天真是個大災難。我在英文課被點名，而且我還不懂老師問的問題。

college

【`kalɪdʒ】

n. [C] 學院；大學

傳統上大學是university，研究所是graduate school。大學生是college student或者是undergraduate。

- graduate 【`grædʒʊ,et】 vt., vi. 畢業
  【`grædʒʊɪt】 n. [C] 畢業生
- undergraduate 【,ʌndɚ`grædʒʊɪt】 n. [C] 大學畢業生

例句

Ava became an engineer after college.
亞娃在大學畢業之後成為了一位工程師。

Anthony is a college student.
安東尼是一位大學生。

會話

A: Are you applying to college?
你正在申請大學嗎？

B: Yes, and it is a tedious procedure.
是的。這真是一個冗長的過程。

lesson

【`lɛsən】
n. [C] 課程

課本裡一課一課就是lesson，而class除了班級的意思之外，也有課程(course)的意思，像是音樂課就是music class，上課中就是in class。同學是classmate。

- class 【klæs】 n. [C] [U] 課，課程；班級
- course 【kors】 n. [C] 課程

例句

Jacob has eight lessons every day.
約伯每天有八堂課。
There are many free Japanese lessons on line.
網路上有許多免費的日語課程。

會話

A: Where is Abigail?
雅比愛兒在哪裡？
B: She is reviewing her lesson in the library.
她在圖書館複習功課。

subject

【`sʌbdʒɪkt】

n. [C] 科目

學校裡把知識(knowledge)分門別類為不同的科目，像是有數學(math)，或是語言(language)，以及科學(science)等學科。

- knowledge 【`nɑlɪdʒ】 n. [U] 知識
- math 【mæθ】 n. [C] 數學
- language 【`læŋgwɪdʒ】 n. [C] 語言
- science 【`saɪəns】 n. [C] [U] 科學

例句

How many subjects are you studying this semester?
你這一學期學多要科目？

會話

A: What's your favorite subject in school?
你在學校最喜歡什麼課目？

B: I like English.
我最喜歡英文。

major

【`medʒɚ】
n. [C] 主修 vi. 主修

大學學位(bachelor's degree)有分主修跟副修(minor)。碩士是master's degree，而博士是PH.D.。

- bachelor 【`bætʃələ】 n. [C] 學士；單身漢
- degree 【dɪ`gri】 n. [C] [U] 學位；程度
- minor 【`maɪnɚ】 n. [C] 副修；vi. 副修
- master 【`mæstɚ】 n. [C] 碩士，大師
- PH.D. =Doctor of Philosophy 博士

例句

Winnie majors in music.
温妮主修音樂。
Emily's major is geography.
愛蜜莉的主修是地理。

會話

A: What do you major in?
你主修什麼？
B: I major in marketing.
我主修行銷。

semester

【sə`mɛstɚ】
n. [C] 學期

像台灣或是美國一樣是一年兩學期的學制，學期是semester。像是英國一樣，一年三個學期的學期是term。學年是academic year。

- term 【tɝm】 n. [C] 一段時間；學期；任期
- academic 【ˌækə`dɛmɪk】 adj. 學術的

例句

Selina failed physics last semester.
賽林娜上學期物裡被當掉。
I had a hard time learning German in the first semester.
在第一學期時，我學習德文有困難。

會話

A: Hey, Allen, what courses will you take this semester?
嘿，亞倫，你這學習要修什麼課啊？
B: Well, I've not decided yet.
呃，我還沒決定好。

textbook

【`tɛkst,bʊk】

n. [C] 教科書，課本

上課前要預習(preview)課本，而下課後要(review)課程，或是讀老師給的課外閱讀(outside reading)。上課記筆記是take notes。

- preview 【`pri,vju】 vt. 預習
- review 【rɪ`vju】 vt. 複習
- note 【not】 n. [C] 筆記；vt. 記筆記

例句

Our textbooks are very informative.
我們的教課書十分有知識性。

Nina was reading a history textbook in the library.
妮娜正在圖書館讀歷史課本。

會話

A: Do you bring your textbooks today?
你們今天有帶課本嗎？

B: Yes, Miss Lin.
有的，林老師。

test

【tɛst】

n. [C] 考試，測驗　vt. 測驗

除了test，我們還有midterm exam(期中考)跟final exam(期末考)。老師上課的隨堂小考則是pop quiz。

- exam 【ɪg`zæm】 n. [C] 考試
- quiz 【kwɪz】 n. [C] 小考

例句

Students in Taiwan have many tests.
在台灣，學生有許多考試。

The engineer tested these machines to make sure they are functional.
那位工程是測試機器以確保它們功能正常。

會話

A: Did you sleep well last night?
你昨晚睡得好嗎？

B: No, I stayed up preparing for the test.
不好，我熬夜準備考試。

grade

Track 087

【gred】

n. [C] 分數；年級

考試得高分是get good grades或是get high score。而作弊是cheat。grade也有級別的意思，所以五年級是the fifth grade。

■ score【skor】n. [C] 分數
■ cheat【tʃit】vt. 作弊；欺騙

例句

Gina got good grades in math.
吉娜數學考了好成績。
Peter is a sixth grader now.
彼得現在是六年級生。

會話

A: You look awful. What's up?
你看起來很糟。怎麼了？
B: I got a poor grade on the final examination.
我期末考考不好。

homework

【 `hom,wɝk 】

n. [U] 作業，回家作業

assignment也是作業，但是是可數名詞。task除了任務的意思，也可以用來指像是實驗(experiment)或實作性質的小作業。而練習題是drill。

- assignment 【 ə`saɪnmənt 】 n. [C] 作業
- task 【 tæsk 】 n. [C] 任務，作業
- experiment 【 ɪk`spɛrəmənt 】 n. [C] 實驗
- drill 【 drɪl 】 n. [C] 練習題

例句

The students handed in their homework to their teacher.
學生把作業交給老師。

I'll play computer games after I finish my homework.
我寫完作業之後會打電動。

會話

A: What are you writing?
你在做什麼？

B: I am doing my homework for biology class.
我在做我生物課的作業。

research

【rɪ`sɝtʃ】

vt. 做研究　n. [U] 研究

做研究我們可以說conduct research。

■ conduct【kən`dʌkt】vt. 執行

例句

The research team conducted a survey in the university.
研究團隊在大學裡坐了一項調查。

The professor's research project was awarded.
這位教授的研究計畫獲得獎項。

會話

A: What do you think about the use of animals for medical research?
對於用動物來做醫學研究，你的看法是什麼？

B: I don't like it. It is cruel.
我不喜歡這樣。這很殘忍。

computer

【kəm`pjutɚ】

n. [C] 電腦

除了電腦，常見的教具還有影片(video)，CD播放器(CD player)，投影機(projector)以及圖表(chart)。

- video 【`vɪdɪ,o】 n. [C] 錄影，錄影節目；錄影機
- player 【`pleɚ】 n. [C] 播放器
- projector 【prə`dʒɛktɚ】 n. [C] 投影機
- chart 【tʃɑrt】 n. [C] 圖表

例句

Fanny helps her daughter install some computer software.
芬妮幫她妹妹安裝了一些電腦軟體。

My computer doesn't work.
我的電腦不能動了。

會話

A: My computer screen just went black!
我的電腦螢幕畫面突然消失不見了！

B: Poor you.
你真可憐。

uniform

【`junə,fɔrm】
n. [C] 制服

在台灣，高中職以下的學校還是有服儀規定(dress code)，要求學生要穿制服。早年的髮禁則叫作hair ban。

- code 【kod】 n. [C] 碼
- ban 【bæn】 n. [C] 禁令

例句

Henry looks handsome in his new uniform.
亨利穿上新制服看起來很帥氣。
All the staff in this hotel is in uniform.
飯店裡的員工全都穿上制服。

會話

A: Do you have to wear school uniforms?
你們要穿學校制服嗎？
B: No, we can wear whatever we like to school.
不用。我們可以穿任何我們想要穿的去上學。

play

【ple】

vt., vi. **玩，遊戲**　n. [C] [U] **玩，遊戲，戲劇**

玩遊戲(game)最能為生活帶來娛樂，玩家則是player。

■ player **【`pleɚ】** n. [C] **玩家，選手**

例句

Zoe likes to play video games in her free time.
佐伊喜歡在閒暇時玩電動遊戲。

All work and no play makes Jack a dull boy.
只是工作而不遊戲，會使人變得遲鈍。

會話

A: Do you like to play volleyball?
　你喜歡打排球嗎？

B: No, but I like to play golf.
　不喜歡，但我喜歡打高爾夫球。

entertain

【ˌɛntɚˋten】

vt., vi. 娛樂

許多遊戲都可以娛樂我們的身心，帶來樂趣(fun)。entertainer是娛樂者，表演者的意思。而娛樂消遣則是entertainment。

- fun 【fʌn】 n. [U] 樂趣，趣味
- entertainer 【ˌɛntɚˋtenɚ】 n. [C] 娛樂人員
- entertainment 【ˌɛntɚˋtenmənt】 n. [U] 娛樂

例句

The clown entertained the kids in the amusement park.
那個小丑娛樂遊樂園的孩子們。

Watching TV is a popular means of entertainment.
看電視是常見的娛樂。

會話

A: What do you think of this program?
你覺得這個節目如何？

B: Not bad. The comedian entertained the audience well.
不錯啊。這個喜劇演員很能娛樂觀眾。

hobby

【`hɑbɪ】

n. [C] 嗜好

許多人會在工作之餘培養嗜好，興趣是interest，消遣是pastime，而娛樂活動有另一種講法是recreation。

- interest 【`ɪntərɪst】 n. [C] 興趣
- pastime 【`pæs,taɪm】 n. [C] 消遣
- recreation 【,rɛkrɪ`eʃən】 n. [U] 娛樂

例句

Collecting stamps is Kim's hobby.
收集郵票是金的嗜好。

Many people cultivate hobbies to kill time.
許多人培養嗜好以排遣時間。

會話

A: Do you have any hobbies?
你有任何嗜好嗎？

B: Yes, I like dancing.
有啊，我喜歡跳舞。

movie

【`muvɪ】
n. [C] [U] 電影

除了看電視，看電影也是現代人的娛樂選擇。電影的其他講法是film或是cinema。cinema也有電影院的意思。電影院也可以說movie theater。

- film 【fɪlm】 n. [C] 電影，軟片，膠捲
- cinema 【`sɪnəmə】 n. [C] 電影；電影院
- theater 【`θɪətɚ】 n. [C] 戲院

例句

Emily likes to watch horror movies in her leisure time.
愛蜜麗喜歡在閒暇之餘看恐怖電影。

The James Bond film series is very popular worldwide.
007電影系列很受全世界歡迎。

會話

A: Would you like to go to a movie?
你想去看 影嗎？

B: Sure. Let's go.
好啊，走吧。

perform

【pə`fɔrm】

vt. 表演

無論是電視，電影或戲劇(drama)，都會提供許多表演讓我們欣賞。表演者是performer，演出或表演是performance，而節目是program。

- drama 【`drɑmə】 n. [C] [U] 戲劇
- performer 【pə`fɔrmə】 n. [C] 表演者
- performance 【pə`fɔrməns】 n. [C] [U] 表演
- program 【`progræm】 n. [C] 節目

例句

Those students will perform a show in the auditorium.
那些學生明天將會在禮堂表演節目。

Vivian enjoys performing onstage.
薇薇安喜歡在台上表演。

會話

A: What do you think of the show?
你覺得這個表演如何？

B: I like the actor's professional performance.
我喜歡這個演員專業的演出。

Internet

【`ɪntə-,nɛt】
n. [U] 網際網路

二十一世紀人類的新娛樂，應該就是上網了(surf the Internet)吧！Internet也可以簡稱Net，線上的是online，所以線上遊戲是online game。而網站是website。

- surf 【sɝf】 vi., vt. 衝浪，上網
- online 【`ɑn,laɪn】 adj., adv. 線上的，線上地
- website 【`wɛb,saɪt】 n. [C] 網站

例句

Surfing the Internet is Mandy's main leisure time activity.
上網是曼蒂主要的休閒活動。

The topic of this seminar is Internet security.
這場座談會的主題是網路安全。

會話

A: Do you know where the nearest Internet café is?
你知道最近的網咖在哪兒？

B: Just go two blocks and you will see one.
你只要走過兩個街區，然後就會看到一間。

exercise

【`ɛksə,saɪz】
n. [C] [U] 運動，鍛鍊；練習題 vt., vi. 鍛鍊，運動

做運動是許多人的休閒活動。exercise就是運動，練習的意思。而sport也是運動，但是指的是運動項目或是活動等，像是運動會就叫作sports event。鍛練身體也可以用動詞片語work out來表示。

- sport【sport】n. [U] [C] 運動
- work out v. phr. 鍛鍊，運動

例句

Aerobics is one of the healthiest forms of exercise.
有氧舞蹈是最健康的鍛鍊身體項目之一。

My grandfather exercised to keep his body and brain healthy.
我祖父運動以保持身體跟大腦的健康。

會話

A: Do you have time for exercise every day?
你每天有時間運動嗎？

B: Yes, I spend 20 minutes jogging in the park.
有啊，我每天花20分鐘在公園跑步。

practice

Track 094

【ˋpræktɪs】

vt., vi. 練習　n. [C] [U] 練習

反覆不斷的練習，我們可以用practice來表示，要注意當它是及物動詞的時候，後面只能接名詞。

例句

Practice makes perfect.
熟能生巧。

Robert practices playing the piano three hours a day.
羅伯特一天練琴三小時。

會話

A: My English is poor.
我英文不好。

B: I think you need more conversation practice.
我想你需要多一些會話練習。

run

【rʌn】

vt., vi. 跑步 n. [C] 跑步

跑步是人們最熟悉的運動之一。jog是慢跑，sprint是快跑，而marathon是馬拉松式長跑。而另一種常見的運動游泳則是swim。

- jog 【dʒag】 vi., n. [C] 慢跑
- sprint 【sprɪnt】 vi., n. [C] 快跑
- marathon 【`mærə,θan】 n. [U] 馬拉松

例句

A dog was running after a stranger.
一隻狗追著一個陌生人。

Charlie ran six miles yesterday.
查理昨天跑了六英里路。

會話

A: You looked tired. Are you OK?
你看起很累。你還好嗎？

B: I've just run 5 km.
我剛跑完五公里。

game

【gem】

n. [C] 遊戲；比賽

game除了遊戲的意思之外，也有運動比賽的意思，像是奧運就是Olympic Games。籃球賽是basketball game，棒球賽是baseball game。但是如果是競速類的比賽，我們會用race，像是慢跑賽是jogging race。而靜態的比賽是contest，像是作文比賽writing contest。

- basketball 【`bæskɪt,bɔl】 n. [C] 籃球
- baseball 【`bes,bɔl】 n. [C] 棒球
- race 【res】 n. [C] 比賽
- contest 【`kɑntɛst】 n. [C] 比賽

例句

My family went to a baseball game last night.
我家人昨晚去看一場球賽。

Henry likes playing video games.
亨利喜歡玩電動。

會話

A: What do you do in your spare time?
你空閒時間都做些什麼？

B: I usually play on-line games.
我通常玩線上遊戲。

gym

【dʒɪm】

n. [C] 健身房，體育館

gym是gymnasium的簡稱。健身房也可以說health club。而stadium也是體育館的意思。在健身房裡常見的運動除了跑步之外，還有舉重(weight-lifting)、瑜珈(yoga)、有氧舞蹈(aerobics)。運動完後的三溫暖是sauna。

- club 【klʌb】 n. [C] 俱樂部
- stadium 【`stedɪəm】 n. [C] 體育館；球場
- yoga 【`jogə】 n. [U] 瑜珈
- aerobics 【eə`robɪk】 n. [C] 有氧舞蹈
- sauna 【`saʊnə】 n. [U] 桑拿浴

例句

People living in a city tend to work out in a gym.
住在城市的人傾向去體育館健身。
There is a gym in this hotel.
這間旅館有健身中心。

會話

A: What do you do after work?
你下班都做些什麼？
B: I often go to a gym for a workout.
我常去健身房健身。

gift

【gɪft】

n. [C] 禮物；天賦 vt. 贈送

不管是送禮或收禮都是令人開心的一件事。present也是禮物的意思。請客是treat。“Treat you a dinner.”就是請你吃晚餐的意思。

- present 【`prɛznt】 n. [C] 禮物
- treat 【trit】 vt., n. [C] 請客

例句

Kira received a lot of birthday gifts from her friends.
琪拉從朋友那裡收到許多生日禮物。

Natalie has a gift for music.
娜塔莉有音樂的天賦。

會話

A: Thank you for the gift you gave me. I really like it.
謝謝你送我的禮物。我很喜歡。

B: You are welcome.
別客氣。

art

【ɑrt】

n. [U] 藝術

欣賞藝術也是許多人的嗜好。fine arts是美術，music是音樂，而sculpture是雕刻。藝術家是artist，artifact是手工藝品。

- sculpture 【`skʌlptʃɚ】 n. [U] [C] 雕刻，雕刻品
- artist 【`ɑrtɪst】 n. [C] 藝術工作者
- artifact 【`ɑrtɪ,fækt】 n. [C] 手工藝品

例句

Janet teaches art history in a university.

珍奈特在大學教藝術史。

Many people find it hard to appreciate modern art.

許多人覺得欣賞現代藝術不容易。

會話

A: What do you think of these paintings?

你覺得這些畫如何？

B: Well, I find modern art hard to comprehend.

呃，我覺得現代藝術很難理解。

paint

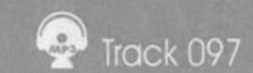

【pent】
vt. 畫畫，漆(顏色)　n. [U] 塗料，顏料

藝術裡最常見的就是視覺藝術。作畫是paint或是draw，而畫作是painting或是drawing，以及picture。picture也有照片(photograph)的意思。

- draw 【drɔ】 vt. 拉；畫畫，塗鴉
- painting 【`pentɪŋ】 n. [C] 畫作
- drawing 【`drɔɪŋ】 n. [C] 畫作
- picture 【`pɪktʃɚ】 n. [C] 畫作，照片

例句

The kid is painting a whale.
那個小孩子正在畫一隻鯨魚。
The room is painted blue.
這個房間漆成藍色的。

會話

A: What are your children doing?
你小孩正在做什麼？
B: They are helping my husband paint the wall white.
他們正在幫我丈夫把牆漆成白色的。

music

【`mjuzɪk】

n. [U] 音樂

聽音樂(listening to music)也是許多人的興趣。唱歌是sing a song。而樂團是band，樂器則是musical instrument。

- sing 【sɪŋ】 vt., vi. 唱歌 動詞三態變化：sing-sang-sung
- song 【sɔŋ】 n. [C] 歌曲
- band 【bænd】 n. [C] 樂團
- musical 【`mjuzɪk!】 adj., n.[C] 音樂的，音樂劇
- instrument 【`ɪnstrəmənt】 n. [C] 工具，器具

例句

Music can influence people's moods.
音樂會影響人的心情。

The students are playing music.
學生正在演奏音樂。

會話

A: What kind of music do you like?
你喜歡什麼音樂？

B: I like pop music.
我喜歡流行樂。

museum

【mju`zɪəm】
n. [C] 博物館，展覽館

欣賞藝術品，通常大家會去博物館或是畫廊(gallery)。演藝廳是performance hall，而音樂廳則是concert hall。

- gallery 【`gælərɪ】 n. [C] 美術館
- concert 【`kɑnsɚt】 n. [C] 音樂會

例句

Olivia works in a fine arts museum.
奧利維亞在美術博物館工作。

There will be a great exhibition in the National Palace Museum.
在故宮將會有一個非常棒的展覽。

會話

A: Which bus goes to the science museum?
哪一輛公車會到科學博物館？

B: You can take bus 201.
你可以搭201公車。

visit

【`vɪzɪt】

vt. 參觀；拜訪　n. [C] 參觀；拜訪

訪問的人、參觀者，或是來拜訪的人都可以成為visitor。遊客中心是visitor's center。visitor's book是訪客登記簿。

■ visitor【`vɪzɪtɚ】n. [C] 訪客，參觀者

例句

Ian visits his parents in the country once a week.
伊安每周會探望一次他住在鄉下的雙親。
This is Helen's first visit to Greece.
這是海倫第一次到訪希臘。

會話

A: What country do you want to visit most?
你最想參訪哪一個國家啊？
B: Japan, because I like Japanese culture.
日本，因為我喜歡日本文化。

celebrate

【`sɛlə,bret】

vt., vi. 慶祝

在特殊的節日(holiday)或是慶典(festival)，人們會大肆慶祝表示喜悅。慶祝活動是celebration。另外許多人也會特意去國外渡假(spend the vacation)來去慶祝一些特別的國外節慶。

- holiday 【`hɑlə,de】 n. [C] 假日
- festival 【`fɛstəv!】 n. [C] 節日，慶祝活動
- celebration 【,sɛlə`breʃən】 n. [C] [U] 慶祝，慶典
- vacation 【ve`keʃən】 n. [C] 假期

例句

Neil's girlfriend bought him a birthday cake to celebrate his birthday.
尼爾的女友幫他買了個生日蛋糕慶祝他生日。

The basketball team held a party to celebrate their victory.
那個籃球隊舉辦了一個晚宴來慶祝他們的勝利。

會話

A: How will you celebrate Tom's birthday?
你們會如何慶祝湯姆的生日。

B: We'll throw a party for him.
我們會幫他舉辦一場派對。

pet

【pɛt】

n. [C] 寵物　vt. 寵愛，愛撫

養寵物也是嗜好之一。常見的寵物有：小狗(puppy)、小貓(kitten)、魚(fish)、鳥(bird)、或是小白兔(rabbit)。寵物生病則會去看獸醫(veterinarian)。

■ veterinarian【ˏvɛtərəˋnɛrɪən】n. [C] (=vet) 獸醫

例句

Fanny kept a kitten as her pet.
芬妮養了一隻貓當寵物。

The mother was gently petting her baby.
媽媽輕柔地愛撫她的寶寶。

會話

A: Jimmy, what are you doing?
吉米，你在做什麼？

B: I am playing with my pet dog.
我在跟我的寵物狗玩耍。

worship

【`wɝʃɪp】

vt., vi. 膜拜；崇拜

許多人會崇拜偶像(idol)明星當做嗜好，也有人會去廟(temple)裡拜拜當作興趣、膜拜、崇敬就是用動詞worship表示。教堂是church。朝拜者就是worshiper。粉絲是fans。

- idol 【`aɪd!】 n. [C] 偶像
- temple 【`tɛmp!】 n. [C] 寺院
- church 【tʃɝtʃ】 n. [C] 教堂
- worshiper 【`wɝʃɪpɚ】 n. [C] 膜拜者

例句

Matthew worships Mazu, the Goddess of the Sea.
馬修敬拜海上女神，媽祖。

Many people worship money in this modern world.
現代社會裡，許多人崇拜金錢。

會話

A: Which idol would you like to spend a day with?
你想要跟哪一個偶像度過一天？

B: Beckham. I worship him a lot.
貝克漢吧！我很崇拜他。

gamble

【`gæmb!】

vt., vi. 賭博 n. [C] 賭博

賭博是一個不良嗜好。賭徒是gambler。在國外，人們可以去賭場(casino)賭博。其他的不良嗜好是沉迷購物或是酗酒。購物狂是shopaholic，而酒鬼是alcoholic。

- gambler 【`gæmb!ɚ】 n. [C] 賭徒
- casino 【kə`sino】 n. [C] 賭場
- shopaholic 【,ʃɑpə`hɔlɪk】 n. [C] 購物狂
- alcoholic 【,ælkə`hɔlɪk】 n. [C] 酗酒者

例句

My uncle in England gambles heavily on the horses.
我在英國的叔叔在賽馬上投了很多賭注。

The beggar gambled away all his money when he was young.
哪個乞丐在年輕時賭光了它所有的錢。

會話

A: Why does Mike gamble?
為什麼麥可賭博？

B: Because he needs a lot of money within a short time.
因為他短時間內需要錢。

lottery

【`latərɪ】

n. [C] 彩券，彩票

玩彩券(play the lottery)也是許多人的興趣之一。中獎是win the lottery，而中頭彩是hit the jackpot。

■ jackpot【`dʒæk,pat】n. [U] 累積獎金

例句

Do you play the lottery?
你玩彩券嗎？
Kate bought a lot of lottery tickets last night.
凱特昨晚買了許多彩券。

會話

A: If you won the lottery, how would you spend the money?
要是你贏了彩券，你會怎麼花這些錢？
B: I would save it.
我會把它存起來。

smoke

【smok】

n. [U] 煙；煙霧 vi., vt. 吸菸；冒煙

老菸槍是heavy smoker。吸菸久了很可能會得肺癌(lung cancer)，所以要戒菸(quit smoking)。二手煙是secondhand smoke。香菸是cigarette。

- lung 【lʌŋ】 n. [C] 肺
- cancer 【\`kænsɚ】 n. [C] [U] 癌，惡性腫瘤
- quit 【kwɪt】 vt., vi. 放棄；停止
- secondhand 【\`sɛkəndhænd】 adj. 第二手的
- cigarette 【ˌsɪgə\`rɛt】 n. [C] 香菸

例句

There's no smoke without fire.
無風不起浪。

The sailor smoked a pipe.
這個水手用菸斗吸菸。

會話

A: Would you mind if I smoke here?
你介意我在這裡吸菸嗎？

B: Well, yes. Please move to the smoking car if you want to smoke, please.
呃，我介意。如果你想吸菸的話，請到吸菸車廂去。

addict

【ə`dɪkt】

vt. 使沉溺，使成癮　n. [C] 上癮的人

許多人玩嗜好久了就成癮。addition是上癮。上癮的是addictive。addict也有上癮的人的意思。

- addition 【ə`dɪʃən】 n. [C] 上癮，入迷
- addictive 【ə`dɪktɪv】 adj. 上癮的
- addict 【`ædɪkt】 n. [C] 上癮的人

例句

Many teenagers are addicted to online games.
許多青少年對網路遊戲上癮成迷。

Betty is a drug addict.
貝蒂是一個吸毒上癮的人。

會話

A: Are you an Internet addict?
你是一個喜歡上網的人嗎？

B: Well, I think I am.
嗯，我想我是。

donate

【`donet】
vt. 捐贈，捐款

去當義工(volunteer)，也是一種嗜好。藉由捐錢，捐時間給慈善機構(charity)，讓愛傳出去。

- volunteer 【ˌvɑlənˋtɪr】 vt., n. [C] 志願，志願者
- charity 【ˋtʃærətɪ】 n. [C] [U] 慈善機構，慈愛

例句

That vendor donated a lot of money to the charities.
那個小販捐了許多錢給慈善機構。
Gina donated books to the library.
吉娜捐錢給圖書館。

會話

A: Do you want to donate blood?
你要捐血嗎？
B: Sure. Let's go.
好啊，走吧。

activity

【æk`tɪvətɪ】

n. [C] 活動

參加活動是許多人的興趣。戶外活動是outdoor activity，室內活動是indoor activity。派對(party)是近年來年輕人喜歡的室內活動。

- outdoor 【`aʊt,dor】 adj. 露天的，戶外的
- indoor 【`ɪn,dor】 adj. 室內的
- party 【`partɪ】 n. [C] 派對，宴會

例句

Quincy is very athletic. He loves outdoor sports.
昆西十分活躍。他很喜歡室外運動。

The amusement park offers many recreational activities.
這個遊樂園提供了許多休閒活動。

會話

A: My life is so boring.
我的生活好無聊喔。

B: Why not take part in some activities after work? It will do you good.
何不參加在下班後參加些活動？這會對你有益處。

PART THREE IN TRAVELLING

旅行最急用

Chapter 3

call

【kɔl】

vt. 打電話　n. [C] (一通)電話

call是一個好用的字，除了可以當名詞用來表示一通電話之外，還可以當動詞表示打電話。除了call之外，ring(鈴聲)跟phone(電話)也可以用來表示打電話跟一通電話之意。

■ ring【rɪŋ】vt. 鈴響；n. [C] 鈴響聲

例句

Jason called Jane last night.
傑森昨晚打電話給珍妮。

The student made a long-distance call to Korea.
那個學生打長途電話到韓國。

會話

A: This is Dave calling. Is Mary in the office?
嗨，這裡是戴夫。瑪莉在辦公室嗎？

B: Yes, this is Mary.
是的，我是瑪莉。

dial

【`daɪəl】

vt. 撥(電話)給；打電話

除了call跟ring之外，dial也可以當作打電話的意思。不同的是，dial的原本意思是撥打電話號碼。

例句

I am afraid that you dialed the wrong number.
我想你打錯的電話了。
Mary dialed Paris directly.
瑪莉直撥巴黎。

會話

A: How do I dial Taipei?
我要怎麼打電話到台北？
B: If you are calling from outside Taipei, make sure you dial 02 in front of the number.
如果你是從台北以外的地方撥號，記得電話號碼之前要加02。

contact

【`kantækt】

vt. 與…接觸；與…聯繫　n. [U] 接觸，聯絡

要跟友人保持聯繫，除了常用的keep in contact之外，我們也可以說keep in touch。此外我們常說的通訊錄，在英文會用contacts表示。而因為隱形眼鏡有跟眼睛接觸，所以叫做contact lens。

■ lens【lɛnz】n. [C] 鏡片，透鏡

例句

Please feel free to contact me if you have any questions.
如果你有任何疑問，請聯絡我。

They still kept in contact even though they were separated.
即便他們分開了，他們仍然保持聯絡。

會話

A: How can I contact you?
我可以怎麼連絡你？

B: You can always contact me on 776-5568.
你可以撥776-5568聯絡我。

wait

【wet】

vi. 等，等待

wait這一個字是不及物動詞，所以我們要說等待某人(或事物)時，別忘了要這麼說：I am waiting for you.

例句

Henry is waiting to have a word with you.
亨利正在等著要跟你説話。
The students are waiting for the school bus.
學生們正在等校車。

會話

A: This is Emily speaking. Is Eric in?
我是愛蜜麗。艾利克在嗎？
B: I'll put you through. Please wait for a moment.
我馬上為你接通，請稍候。

answer

【`ænsɚ】 vt. 回答，答覆；接(電話)，應(門)
n. [C] 答案；回答，答覆

answer除了是常見的「答案」的意思之外，用在打電話跟應門，都有回應的意思。

例句

Do you know the answer to this math question?
你知道這道數學題的答案嗎？

Did anyone answer the phone?
有人回覆這通電話了嗎？

會話

A: Hello, this is Melissa speaking.
你好，我是瑪莉莎。

B: Uh…if you don't mind, please call back and leave a message on the answering machine. I am kind of busy right now. I will call you back as soon as possible.
呃…要是你不介意的話，請再打一次並留言在電話答錄機裡。我現在有點兒忙。我會儘快回撥。

message

【`mɛsɪdʒ】

vt. 通知，聯繫 n. [C] 口信，訊息；消息

在手機還沒發明的年代，message只有訊息或是留言的意思。在手機發明之後，簡訊就是text message。到了現在，app跟line都可以當成動詞表示用WhatsApp跟Line來留訊息給對方。

■ text【tɛkst】n. [C] 文本；vt. 傳簡訊

例句

Kelvin just sent a message, saying that he was not able to come here tonight.
凱文剛傳了個訊息給我，說他今晚沒辦法到這裡了。
Would you like to leave a message?
你要留言嗎？

會話

A: Leo is out on his lunch break right now. Can I take a message?
里歐出去吃午飯了, 你要留言嗎？

B: No, thank you. I will call him.
不用了，謝謝你。我會再打電話給他。

number

【`nʌmbɚ】

n. [C] 數，數字；號碼

在數學裡，number是「數字」或是「號碼」的意思。這一個字的應用範圍很廣，用在地址，它指的是「門牌號碼」；而在電話英文裡，就是「電話號碼」了。而分機號碼，則會用到extension這一個字。

■ extension【ɪk`stɛnʃən】n. [C] 電話分機

例句

The number of the students in this class is 37.
這班的學生數是37人。
Sandy lives at number 11 Walnut Street.
珊蒂住在胡桃街11號。

會話

A: Hello, is Fiona there?
嗨，費歐娜在嗎？
B: I'm sorry. I'm afraid you've got the wrong number.
抱歉，恐怕你打錯電話了。

phone

【fon】

vt. 打電話給，打電話 n. [U] 電話

電話是telephone，也可以簡稱phone。不過現在phone這一個字的應用範圍很廣，它還可能指cell phone或是 mobile phone（手機），或者是smart phone或是super phone（智慧型手機）。

- cell 【sɛl】 n. [C] 單人小室；蜂巢
- mobile 【`mobɪl】 adj. 可移動的

例句

Lily phoned me last night.
麗麗昨晚打電話給我。
Jack spoke to me by phone this morning.
今天早上傑克跟我通話。

會話

A: Hello, is Henry there?
嗨，亨利在嗎？
B: He is on his business trip. Do you have his cell phone number?
他出差中喔。你有它手機號碼？

busy

【`bɪzɪ】

adj. 忙碌的，繁忙的；(指電話線)正被佔用的，不通的

當我們很忙的時候，我們會說I am busy.。而電話打不通時，我們常常會聽到The line is busy.，表示「線路正在忙線中」。

■ line【laɪn】n. [C] 線；電話線

例句

The manager is busy with the new project.
經理正忙著新方案。
The phone is busy. Please try again later.
電話正在忙線中。請稍候再撥。

會話

A: Linda, can you answer the phone? I am busy.
琳達，你能不能去接電話？我正在忙。
B: Sure.
好啊。

available

【ə`veləb!】

adj. 可用的，在手邊的；有空的，可與之聯繫的

當某個東西對我們而言是可取得的，我們會說It is available.。所以，在電話英語裡，當你要連絡的人是有空跟你說話時，我們也會說He is available.。要注意的是，當某個人剛好目前是沒有男女朋友，是可以追求的狀態是，我們也會說：She is available.。

例句

Is there any dictionary available around?
附近有字典嗎？
The manager is available now.
經理現在可以跟你說話。

會話

A: Can I talk to Paul?
保羅在嗎？
B: He's not available right now. Would you like to leave a message?
他不在，你要留言嗎？

fax

【fæks】

vt. 用傳真機傳輸 n. [C] 傳真機

除了電話跟電腦之外，傳真機也是常用的通訊方式。在還沒有傳真機或是電子郵件(e-mail)來傳遞書面訊息前，telegram(電報)是人們用來傳遞telegraphic message(電報消息)的工具。

例句

Please fax me these documents as soon as possible.
請儘快傳真給我這些文件。

The fax machine is available in this hotel.
這件旅店有提供傳真服務。

會話

A: Can you help me with the fax machine? It doesn't work.
你可以幫我修一下傳真機嗎？它壞了。

B: Sure. I will come up around 1:30.
好啊，我一點過去看看。

soon

【sun】

adv. 不久，很快地

表示動作迅速或者是快速，英文裡有許多同義詞如fast, quickly, soon, promptly或是swiftly等等。然而電話英語裡，回電迅速，常用的副詞則是soon這一個字；而在回信方面，除了soon，另一常用的副詞則是promptly。

■ promptly【pramptlɪ】adv. 迅速地

例句

Mike is not around, but I am sure he will come back soon.
麥可現在不在，但是我確定他一會兒就會回來。
I will call you back soon.
我會馬上回電給你。

會話

A: Hi, this is Ron. I'm either away from my desk, or on the phone. Please leave a message and I'll get right back to you as soon as possible.
嗨！我是容恩。我現在不是不在辦公室裡，就是在電話中。請留言。我會儘快回你電話。

mail

【mel】

vi. 郵寄　n. [U] 郵遞，郵政；n. [C] 郵件

除了電話跟傳真，通訊的另一種方式就是寄信了。從古代到現代，書信往返甚至是電郵往來，我們都可以用mail這一個字。如果要更明確做區分，email就是特別指電子信件了。而信件，我們則可以用letter表示。

■ letter【`lɛtɚ】n. [C] 信，郵件

例句

Diana mailed the package to John.
黛安娜寄了個包裹給約翰。

Linda received some mails this morning.
琳達今天早上收到了一封信。

會話

A: Have you heard from Alan?
你有收到艾倫的消息嗎？

B: He just emailed me last night.
他昨晚才寄電子郵件給我。

hear from

vt. 聽到…的消息；收到…的信

無論是接電話(pick up a phone call)或是收信(receive a letter)，在訊息(message)裡，我們都會聽到他人的消息。在英文裡我們可以用hear from這個動詞片語表示在電話裡或書信裡「聽到…的消息」。而廣義的「聽說」則是用hear about。

例句

I've not heard from you for a while.
我好一陣子沒有收到你的消息了。
I am looking forward to hearing from you.
我期待收到你的消息。

會話

A: I have not heard from Kim since she left for America last summer.
自從金去年暑假去美國後，我都沒有再聽說她的消息了。
B: Why not write an email to her?
何不寫封電子郵件給他？

time

【taɪm】

n. [U] 時間　vt. 安排…的時間

每個國家對於約會守時(punctual)的習慣不同，但是時間觀念卻是人人都要有的。尤其是在旅行中，各個國家的時區(time zone)不同，對於時間的精確掌握更是重要。

■ punctual【`pʌŋktʃʊəl】adj. 守時的

例句

Time is money.
時間是金錢。

The train to Taichung is timed to depart at 6:30.
往台中的火車預定6點半離開。

會話

A: What time is it?
現在幾點了？

B: It is ten past five.
現在五點十分。

hour

【aʊr】

n. [C] [U] 小時；時刻，時間

hour這一個字除了有小時的意思之外，也有指特定時間的意思，例如，office hours指的就是「上班時間」，而visiting hours指的就是「探病時間」。相關字o'clock是副詞，指的是整點鐘的意思。

- o'clock【ə`klɑk】adv. …點鐘
- clock【klɑk】n. [C] 時鐘

例句

It took Eunice three hours to solve that math problem!
解這道數學題花了尤里斯三個小時。
Please contact me during the office hours.
請在上班時間時聯絡我。

會話

A: When will we reach the destination?
我們何時會抵達目的地？
B: About half an hour.
大約半小時吧。

minute

【`mɪnɪt】

n. [C] 分鐘，一會兒，片刻

minute除了有分鐘的意思，也有片刻，頃刻(moment，instant)的意思。在時鐘上看到的分針，英文上會說minute hand。同理，hour hand就是時針。而一秒鐘則會用second來表示。

- moment 【`momənt】 n. [C] 瞬間，片刻
- instant 【`ɪnstənt】 n. [C] 瞬間，片刻；adj. 立刻的，即刻的
- second 【`sɛkənd】 n. [C] 秒

例句

It takes five to ten minutes to make a bowl of instant noodles.
泡一碗泡麵需要5到10分鐘。

Stay here! Mom will be back in a minute.
待在那兒！媽媽一會兒就回來。

會話

A: Hello, this is James. May I speak to Carol?
嗨，我是詹姆士。卡羅在嗎？

B: Yes, one moment please. I'll get her for you.
在的，請等一下，我去叫她來。

day

【de】

n. [C] 一天，日；白天

一日可以說a day，而一日中的白天也是用day這個字表示。day也可以用來表示特定節日，例如Mothers' Day(母親節)，Charismas Day(聖誕節)，或是Valentine's Day(情人節)。

例句

What day is today? Today is Tuesday.
今天星期幾？今天是星期二。

Karen stays at home during the day and goes to work at night.
凱倫白天待在家而晚上出門工作。

會話

A: What day is today?
今天星期幾？

B: It's Sunday.
今天禮拜天。

date

【det】

n. [C] 日期，日子；約會　vt. 在…註明日期

跟day比較起來，date這一個字更精準地表示「日期」。當人們問What date時，通常回答都會把日期、月份，甚至年份都回答出來。此外，date也有男女約會之意，例如blind date指的就是相親，而speed dating就是近年流行的閃電約會。

例句

What date is the National Day?
國慶日是幾月幾號？

Please date our appointment in your schedule.
請在你的行事曆註記上我們的約會。

會話

A: Do you know the exact date of Thanksgiving this year?
你知道今年感恩節確切是幾號嗎？

B: No, but let me check the calendar.
不知道耶，但是讓我查查月曆吧。

week

【wik】

n. [C] 週；一星期

日子一天一天過，很快的工作日(week days，常指周一到周五)結束，就會到令人愉快周末(weekend)，而一星期，我們會說a week，而每周一期的周刊，我們會說weekly。

■ weekly【`wiklɪ】n. [C] 週刊；adv.每週地

例句

Nick goes jogging twice a week.
尼克每週慢跑兩次。

The museum is open 10 to 5 on weekdays.
博物館周間早上10點到下午5點開門。

會話

A: You look tired. What's the matter with you?
你看起來很疲憊。怎麼了？

B: I've been preparing for the job interview next week.
我最近在準備下周的工作面試。

year

【jɪr】

n. [C] 年，一年；年度

除了周(week)是會是我們在月曆(calendar)上看到的時間度量單位，月份(month)年份(year)也會是我們常用到的字。而年報或是月刊，我們會說yearly以及monthly。

- yearly 【`jɪrlɪ】 n. [C] 年報；adv. 每年地
- month 【mʌnθ】 n. [C] 月，一個月
- monthly 【`mʌnθlɪ】 n. [C] 月刊；adv. 每月地

例句

Tom did not come home this year.
湯姆今年都沒有回家。
There are twelve months in one year.
一年裡有十二個月。

會話

A: How long will you stay in France?
你會在法國待多久？
B: I am going to stay here for at least one year.
我將在這兒待上至少一年。

today

【tə`de】

n. [U] 今天 adv. 今天

day指的是日子，而today指的就是今天，而tonight是今晚。如果我們要再細分「現在」或者是「當下」，則會用now或是at present。

- now 【naʊ】 adv. 現在
- present 【`prɛznt】 adj. 現在的

例句

Today is Chris's birthday.
今天是克里斯的生日。
Sam did not go to the office today because he is sick.
山姆今天因為生病而沒去上班。

會話

A: How are you today?
你今天如何？
B: I am fine. Thank you.
我很好，謝謝。

yesterday

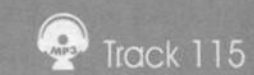
Track 115

【`jɛstɚde】

n. [U] 昨天　adv. 昨天

「前天」會說the day before yesterday，「前些天」是the other day，「上周」是last week，而「上個月」是last month。要記得，當使用這些字時，句子裡的動詞時態要用過去式。

■ last【læst】adj. 上一個的，之前的

例句

Oliver encountered his high school classmate in a café yesterday.

奧利佛昨天在咖啡館裡邂逅他的高中同學。

Mimi went to the movie with her family the other day.

前些天咪咪跟他家人去看電影。

會話

A: Where were you yesterday?

你昨天去那兒了？

B: I went to the book fair.

我去逛書展了。

tomorrow

【tə`mɔro】

n. [U] 明天　adv. 明天

「後天」是the day after tomorrow，「下一周」是next week，而「下個月」是next month。要記得用到這些字時，動詞要跟著will(將會)這一個助動詞一起連用。

■ next【`nɛkst】adj. 下一個的

例句

My parents will leave for Japan tomorrow.
我爸媽下禮拜會去日本。

Peggy's wedding will take place the day after tomorrow.
佩姬的婚禮將在後天舉行。

會話

A: Will you be free tomorrow?
你明天有空嗎？

B: Yes. What's up?
有啊，怎麼了嗎？

morning

【`mɔrnɪŋ】

n. [U] [C] 早晨

一天的白晝，是daytime，早晨、清晨則用morning，dawn是清晨破曉時分。morning call是晨喚服務。

■ dawn【dɔn】n. [C] [U] 黎明

例句

William usually has a cup of coffee in the morning.
威廉通常在早上喝一杯咖啡。

The hotel provides wake-up call service.
飯店提供晨喚服務。

會話

A: Good morning. How are you?
早安你好啊。

B: I am fine. Thank you.
我很好，謝謝。

afternoon

【`æftɚ`nun】

n. [U] [C] 下午，午後

正中午吃飯時間，我們常用noon。而過了正中午，我們就會說afternoon。afternoon tea則是下午茶。

■ noon【nun】n. [C] [U] 正午

例句

It is good for you to take a nap in the afternoon.
下午小睡片刻對你有益。

Kate loves to have afternoon tea with her colleagues.
凱特喜歡跟他同事共進下午茶。

會話

A: Are you going to the movie with us?
你要跟我們去看電影嗎？

B: Sorry. I have an appointment with my dentist this afternoon.
抱歉，我今天下午要去看牙醫。

evening

【`ivnɪŋ】

n. [C] [U] 下午，傍晚

在英文中，晚上有兩種：傍晚時分，或是晚上見面打招呼，我們會用evening這一個字；而天黑後，或是晚上道別時，我們會用night。

■ night【naɪt】n. [C] [U] 夜晚，晚上；adj. 夜晚的

例句

I will pick you up in the evening.
我傍晚會來接你。
Graham loves to read novels before he goes to bed at night.
葛蘭喜歡在晚上睡覺前讀些小說。

會話

A: We'll have an evening party. Please come and join us.
我們要開晚會。請你來參加。
B: I'd be glad to.
我很樂意。

recently

【`risəntlɪ】

adv. 最近

同義詞有lately，要注意這個時間副詞常跟動詞完成式連用。

■ lately【`letlɪ】adv. 最近，不久

例句

Sales have dropped recently.
銷售額最近下降了。
What have you been doing recently?
你最近都在做什麼？

會話

A: What have you been doing recently?
你最近都在做什麼？
B: Oh, I've been busy with the new project.
喔，我都在忙著新的專案。

already

【ɔl`rɛdɪ】

adv. 已經

強調動作已經完成，我們會用already這一個時間副詞來加強語氣。其相反詞是yet，表示「還沒有」。另外，just這一個時間副詞表示「剛剛、剛才」要注意這些時間副詞常跟動詞完成式連用。

- yet 【jɛt】 adv. 還沒有
- just 【dʒʌst】 adv. 剛剛，剛才

例句

Tony is already twenty-five years old.
湯米已經二十五歲了。
We have already had our breakfast.
我們已經吃過早餐了。

會話

A: I am sorry for being late for the meeting.
抱歉我開會來晚了。
B: That's OK because the meeting has already been cancelled.
沒關係，反正會議已經取消了。

meanwhile

【`min,hwaɪl】

adv. 同時地，與此同時 n. 其間

兩件事在同時間發生，我們可以用時間副詞meanwhile來表示。同義詞有meantime跟at the same time。

- meantime【`min,taɪm】adv. 同時地；n. 其間
- at the same time adv. phr. 同時地

例句

Amber was in New York for a week, and meanwhile she went on with the work.
安柏在紐約待上一周，同時也持續她的工作。

The flight won't take off for two hours. In the meantime, we can have lunch.
飛機還有兩個小時才要起飛，我們可以在這當中吃午餐。

會話

A: What did you do on your trip to Japan?
你們日本行都做些什麼？

B: We had some business meetings. Meanwhile, we visited some museums.
我們開了些生意上的會議。同時，我們也參觀了些博物館。

while

【hwaɪl】

n. [C] 一陣子，一段時間，一會兒

while當名詞的時候，表示時間「一會兒」的意思。同義詞有period。常見的片語有「有時候」: once in a while以及「一陣子」: in a while。

■ period 【`pɪrɪəd】 n. [C] 期間，一會兒

例句

Hardman visited his parents once in a while.
赫德曼有時候會去探望他的雙親。
I haven't seen William for a while.
我好一陣子沒見到威廉了。

會話

A: Will Chris be back to work?
克里斯還會回來工作嗎？
B: Yes. He is just taking sick leave for a while.
會啊。他只是請一陣子的病假。

forever

【fɚˋɛvɚ】
adv. 永遠地

同義詞有eternally與permanently，反義詞是temporarily，暫時地。

- eternally 【ɪˋtɝnəlɪ】 adv. 永恆地，永遠地
- permanently 【ˋpɝmənəntlɪ】 adv. 永久地，永遠地
- temporarily 【ˋtɛmpə,rɛrəlɪ】 adv. 暫時地

例句

Julie is my best friend forever.
朱麗永遠是我最好的朋友
Nothing lasts forever.
沒有東西會永遠存在。

會話

A: How's your senior high life?
你高中生活如何？
B: It's awesome. I will remember my high school life forever.
很棒，我永遠無法忘記我的高中生活。

hurry

【`hɝɪ】

vt. 使…趕緊，催促 n. [U] 倉忙，匆促

時間如果急了，行動難免匆促，不可緩慢(slow)，而匆匆忙忙的樣子，就是hurry。處於匆忙的狀態就是in a hurry。急忙衝去做某件事，我們還可以用rush。

■ rush【rʌʃ】vt. 衝，奔，急速行動；n. [C] [U] 匆忙

例句

Diana hurried to work because she got up late this morning.
黛安娜因為早上睡過頭，而匆忙趕著上班。

The desperate customer was in a hurry to see the store manager.
這一個絕望的顧客急急忙忙地要見店經理。

會話

A: Are you in a hurry?
你趕時間嗎？

B: Yes, please drive fast.
是的，請開快一點。

fast

【fæst】

adj. 迅速的，快速的 adv. 快速地，快地

表示動作快速，我們可以用fast或是quick以及soon。fast food是速食；fast train是快車。slow(緩慢)是它的相反詞。

- slow 【slo】 adj. 慢的
- slowly 【`slolɪ】 adv. 緩慢地

例句

Learning from doing is a fast way to master a skill.
做中學是精通一個技術的快速方式。
Henry runs fast.
亨利跑得很快。

會話

A: Hey, you are driving too fast!
嘿，你車開太快了！
B: Sorry. I will slow down a bit.
抱歉，我會開慢一點。

late

【let】

adj. 遲的；晚的；最近的 adv. 遲的；晚的；不久前

來不及，遲到了就是用late這一個字；相反地，要是「提早」了，則會用early這一個字。早鳥就叫做early bird。

■ early【`ɝlɪ】adj. 早的，提早的；adv. 早地，提早地

例句

I am so sorry for being late for the meeting.

我很抱歉會議遲到了。

Peter often worked late into the night.

彼得常常工作到深夜。

會話

A: You look awful. Are you OK?

你看起來很糟。你還好嗎？

B: No, I stayed up late finishing this project and feel sleepy now.

不好，我昨夜熬夜完成這個案子，現在很想睡。

schedule

【`skɛdʒʊl】 n. [C] 日程表，時間表，時刻表
vt. 預定；將…列入表中

除了常用表示日程表的名詞意思之外，schedule在車站裡的表示時刻表。持課表也可以說time table。當動詞則有預定(出發)的意思。

■ time table n. [C] 時間表

例句

Thomas is busy and his schedule is tight.
湯瑪士很忙，而且他的行程也很緊湊。
Could you schedule an interview for me?
你可以幫我安排面試的時間嗎？

會話

A: You know what? Our project is ahead of schedule.
你知道嗎，我們的計劃超前進度耶。
B: That's great.
那真是太棒了。

efficient

【ɪˋfɪʃənt】

adj. 有效率的

動作快且能夠在有限的時間之內完成要完成的工作，就是有效率。達成目標就是有效果effective。而動作迅速，則用quick來表達。

- effective 【ɪˋfɛktɪv】 adj. 有效果的
- quick 【kwɪk】 adj. 快的，迅速的；adv. 快的，迅速的

例句

Sean was efficient in his work.
尚恩工作效率高。

She is an efficient secretary.
她是個有效率的秘書。

會話

A: Which car do you recommend?
你推薦哪一台車？

B: How about this one? It is so fuel efficient.
這一台好嗎？它超級省油。

ahead

【ə`hɛd】

adv. 在前，預先，事前

超級有效率的工作者都能在工作截止日之前(deadline)完成工作。在進度之前，我們會說ahead of time或是ahead of schedule。「預先，事前」我們還能說beforehand或是in advance。而落後則是說fall behind schedule。

- behind 【bɪ`haɪnd】 prep. 落後於
- beforehand 【bɪ`for,hænd】 adv. 預先，事先
- in advance adv. 預先，事先

例句

Make sure you make plans ahead.
確認你在事前都先規劃。

The student finished his term paper ahead of time.
學生提前完成他的學期作業。

會話

A: I am sorry for being late for school.
很抱歉我上學遲到了。

B: You should leave a few minutes ahead of time.
你應該提早出門的。

enter

【`ɛntɚ】

vt., vi. 進入

去到一個地方，我們會看到入口是entrance或是entry。入場費就是entrance fee。而這兩個字的動詞就是enter。出口或離開就是exit。

- entrance 【`ɛntrəns】 n. [C] [U] 入口，進入
- entry 【`ɛntrɪ】 n. [C] [U] 入口，進入
- exit 【`ɛksɪt】 vi. 離去，出去；n. [C] 出口

例句

In countries like China and Japan, you have to take off your shoes before entering a house.
像在中國以及日本這樣子的國家，你在進屋之前要脫鞋。

All the students rose when the teacher entered.
當老師進來的時候，所有的學生都起立。

會話

A: Where is Booth 17?
攤位十七號在哪兒？

B: Just enter from the gate, directly go to the second floor, and you will see it on your right.
直接從大門進去，上二樓，然後它就在你的右邊。

pass

【pæs】 vi. 前進；通過；經過；超過
vt. 經過；穿過 n. [C] 通行證

在有些機關單位，進出都需要通行證，通行證就是用pass這一個字，像是護照就叫passport。而通過這一個動詞也就是pass。pass by指的就是「經過」某處，而路人就是passerby。

- passerby 【`pæsɚ`baɪ】 n. [C] 路人，行人
- passport 【`pæs,port】 n. [C] 護照；通行證

例句

Dave passed a bakery when he drove to work in the early morning.
戴夫每天早上開車上班時會經過一間麵包店。
Fanny passed by a church on her way to work.
芬妮上班的路上會經過一間教堂。

會話

A: I need one bus pass.
我要買一張公車卡。
B: Thirty dollars, please.
請給我三十元。

park

【park】

vt., vi. 停放(車輛)　n. [C] 公園；停車場

park是一個很好用的一個字，當它是動詞時，指的就是「泊」車或是停車的意思。而當它是名詞時，指的除了有常用的公園之意，car park指的就是停車場。停車場還可以用parking lot來表示。

例句

Where can I park my car?

我可以在哪裡停車？

There is a car park near the school.

學校附近有一個停車場。

會話

A: Where is the parking lot?

停車場在哪兒？

B: It's just around the corner.

就在角落而已。

cross

【krɔs】

vt. 越過，渡過　vi. 橫越，橫渡

cross除了有常見的「十字架」之意，當它是動詞時，指的是橫越或是渡過某個地方。cross street指的就是十字路口；zebra crossing是斑馬線，而過馬路就是cross the road。但是直直地「穿越」某個地方，我們則會再用through這一個字。

■ through【θru】prep. 穿過，通過

例句

It is kind of Peter to help an old lady cross the road.

彼得很好心地幫助一個老太太過馬路。

They crossed through the forest.

她們橫越過一個森林。

會話

A: How can I get to the museum?

我要怎麼到博物館？

B: Cross the street by going underground and then you will see it on your left.

走地下道過街，然後你就會看到它在左邊。

miss

【mɪs】

vt. 未趕上，錯過

時間要是不小心沒有掌控好，就會miss（錯過）火車，客運或是飛機。但是如果努力一點趕上了，我們則會用catch up with來表示。

例句

Sandra missed the school bus because she overslept this morning.
珊卓因為今天早上睡過頭而錯過校車。

Frank missed going to the party last week.
法蘭克上周沒有去那個宴會。

會話

A: I almost missed the train this morning.
我差點錯過今天早上的火車。

B: You should have left earlier.
你該早點出門的。

depart

【dɪ`part】

vi. 起程, 出發; 離開, 離去

除了常用的leave(離開),depart這一個動詞,或是它的名詞departure,更常出現在客運站,火車站或是機場來表示客運,火車或是飛機即將起程離站。departure time指的就是離站時間。

■ departure【dɪ`partʃɚ】n. [C] [U]

例句

The train is scheduled to depart at 9 o'clock.
這班火車預計九點整離站出發。
The flight's departure is on schedule.
這班飛機準時起程。

會話

A: What time would you like to depart?
您預計什麼時間出發?
B: I hope I can depart before noon.
我希望中午之前能出發。

arrive

【ə`raɪv】

vi. 到達；到來

除了reach，班機、火車或是我們抵達某處，都可以用arrive這一個動詞表示。更常出現在客運站，火車站或是機場來表示客運，火車或是飛機即將抵達的是它的名詞arrival。arrival lobby指的就是機場的入境大廳。

■ arrival【ə`raɪv!】n. [U] 到達；到來，達到

例句

Jean arrived home early this evening.
琴今天傍晚提早到家。

Jason waited for his cousin at the arrival lobby.
傑森在入境大廳等他的堂弟。

會話

A: What time does the earliest bus arrive?
最早班火車何時抵達？

B: Around five thirty.
大約五點三十。

delay

【dɪˋle】

vt. 耽擱；延誤

火車、班機或客運「準時」出發或抵達，我們會用on time來表示。in time表示「即時」趕上。然而因為accident（意外）或是其他因素而無法準時抵達，則會用到delay這一個字。

■ accident【ˋæksədənt】n. [C] 事故，意外

例句

The car accident delayed the train for an hour.
車禍使火車延遲了一個小時。
The heavy rain delayed the arrival of the parcel.
大雨延誤了包裹抵達。

會話

A: Why do you delay the homework?
你為什麼遲交作業？
B: Sorry, Miss Lin. I will try to hand it in to you tomorrow.
抱歉林老師。我明天會趕快交出來。

travel

【`træv!】

vi. 旅行　vt. 在…旅行，經過　n. [U] 旅行，遊歷

在外旅遊歷，或是長途的旅行，我們會用travel這一個字。go travelling就是去旅行，traveler指的就是旅行者。同義字還有tour跟trip。短程的行程我們常用trip這一個字表示。

- trip 【trɪp】 n. [C] (短程)旅行
- tour 【tʊr】 n. [C] 旅行，行程

例句

Alice is travelling in Europe.
愛麗絲正在歐洲旅行。

Henry enjoyed his three-day travel in Tokyo very much.
亨利在東京的三日旅行過得很愉快。

會話

A: What do you do, Wendy?
你是做什麼的，温蒂？

B: I work in a travel agency.
我在旅行社工作。

ticket

【`tɪkɪt】

n. [C] 票，券；車票

無論是坐公車(bus)、火車或是飛機，都要買票。買票我們可以說buy a ticket。如果是「預定」票券，則用book a ticket來表示。

■ book【bʊk】vt. 預約，預定

例句

You can buy the ticket at the front gate.
你可以在大門處買票。

It is convenient to book a ticket online.
在網上訂票很方便。

會話

A: Can I change my one-way ticket to a round-trip ticket?
我可以把單程票改成來回票嗎？

B: Sure. Forty dollars and your one-way ticket, please.
可以的，請給我四十元跟您的單程票。

fare

【fɛr】

n. [C] (交通工具的)票價；車(船)費

票券的費用，我們會用fare或者是它的同義字fee表示。而過站的通行費則會用toll表示。ETC的全名就是electronic toll collector(電子收費系統)。

- fee 【fi】 n. [C] 費用
- toll 【tol】 n. [C] 通行費

例句

Be sure you have enough money for the bus fare.
確保你有帶夠公車票的錢。

How much is the fare?
票價怎麼算？

會話

A: How much is the fare?
車票多少錢？

B: Thirty five, please.
三十五元。

port

【port】

n. [C] 港口

火車有platform（月台）或是station（車站）讓乘客等車，船有port（港口），而飛機則有airport（機場）可以停靠。

- platform 【`plæt,fɔrm】 n. [C] （火車站）月台
- station 【`steʃən】 n. [C] （客運，火車）站
- airport 【`ɛr,port】 n. [C] 機場

例句

The ship will reach the port by noon.
中午前船會抵達港口。

We have to arrive at the airport at 3:30.
我們會在3點半抵達港口。

會話

A: When will the ship arrive?
船何時抵達？

B: The ship will arrive at the port by noon.
船將會在中午前到港。

rent

【rɛnt】

vt., vi. 租 n. [C] [U] 租金，出租費

出外旅遊，出了可以乘坐大眾交通工具(public transportation)之外，你也可以自行租車出遊。汽車出租是car rental，出租費率則是rental rate。

- rental 【`rɛnt!】 n. [C] 租金；出租
- rate 【ret】 n. [C] 價格，費用

例句

I want to rent a car.
我想要租一輛車。

How much is the rent?
租金怎麼算？

會話

A: I would like to rent a car.
我想要租一台車。

B: Here is the inventory of cars. Which one do you like?
這是車子的目錄。你喜歡哪一台？

signal

【`sɪgn!】

n. [C] 標示；交通指示燈

無論在馬路上，或者是在機場，車站裡，我們會看到很多標示來告知(inform)我們在行進時要注意的事項。紅綠燈是traffic lights或是traffic signals。而標示牌或告示牌則會用到sign這一個字。

■ sign【saɪn】n. [C] 標示，招牌

例句

Red light Is used as a danger signal.
紅燈被用來當作危險的標示。
The traffic sign says, "No entry"!
這一個告示牌上寫著:「禁止進入」。

會話

A: Watch out!
小心！
B: Sorry. I forgot to pay attention to the traffic signal.
抱歉。我忘了注意紅綠燈。

lost

【lɔst】

adj. 遺失的，迷路的

旅行中，如果能按著地圖(map)，依照預先規劃好路線(route)好好地行走，同常就不會有get lost(迷路)的問題。

- map 【mæp】 n. [C] 地圖
- route 【rut】 n. [C] 路線

例句

It is hard to find your lost purse in such a big train station.
在這麼大的車站裡很難找到你遺失的錢包。

Excuse me, I am lost. Can you show me the way to the train station?
抱歉，我迷路了。你可以告訴我去火車站的路嗎？

會話

A: Excuse me. I am lost. Can you take me to the police station?
不好意思，我迷路了。你能帶我去警察局嗎？

B: OK.
好的。

arrange

【ə`rendʒ】

vt. 安排，籌備；佈置，整理

出外旅行，最重要的是事前的安排(arrangement)，無論是自助旅行(backpacking)或是套裝行程(package tour)，事前好好地籌畫做功課準沒錯。

■ arrangement【ə`rendʒmənt】n. [C] [U] 安排

例句

Have you arranged for someone to pick you up at the airport?

你已經安排好去機場接你的人了嗎？

My mother had arranged the living room before the guests arrived.

媽媽在客人到之前已經把客廳整理好了。

會話

A: Do you like package tours?

你喜歡套裝行程嗎？

B: Yes. The travel agency will arrange everything for my trip.

喜歡。因為旅行社會幫我安排好一切行程細節。

plane

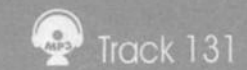

【plen】
n. [C] 飛機

plane的全名是airplane飛機。飛機有很多中，jet是噴射機，helicopter是直升機。是passenger airplane客機。飛機還可以說aircraft。如果要特別指稱航班，則用flight。而乘坐飛機叫做take the airplane。

- jet【dʒɛt】n. [C] 噴射機
- helicopter【`hɛlɪkɑptɚ】n. [C] 直升機
- aircraft【`ɛr,kræft】n. [C] 飛機
- flight【flaɪt】n. [C] (飛機的)班次；(某班次的)飛機；飛機的航程

例句

The plane is about to take off.
這班飛機準備起飛。
Do you know when flight 707 arrives in Taipei?
你知道班機707何時抵達台北嗎？

會話

A: Do you know when flight 401 will arrive?
你知道401班機何時抵達？
B: Hold on. I will check for you.
請稍候，我將為您查詢。

fly

【flaɪ】

vi., vt. 飛，飛行

飛機或是飛禽飛行，用fly，要注意這一個動詞屬於不規則變化fly-flew-flown。飛機起飛則會用take off，降落land這兩個動詞。

■ land【lænd】vt. 降落

例句

Liam will fly to New York tomorrow.

連明天會坐飛機去紐約。

The pilot has flown a passenger airplane for many years.

這個駕駛員駕駛客機已經好多年了。

會話

A: What airline would you like to fly?

您要搭乘哪一家航空公司的飛機？

B: China Airlines.

華航。

seat

【sit】

n. [C] 座，座位 vt. 使就坐

進了飛機機艙(cabin)，就是找座位(seat)坐好。飛機座位等級分成first class(頭等艙)，business class(商務艙)，跟economic class(經濟艙)。座位則分成兩種：window seat(靠窗座位)跟aisle seat(走道座位)。

- class 【klæs】 n. [C] 等級；級別
- cabin 【`kæbɪn】 n. [C] 機艙

例句

Please be seated.
請坐好。

Please fasten your seat belt.
請繫上座位上的安全帶。

會話

A: Hello.
哈囉。

B: Have a seat and drink some tea.
來坐下喝口茶吧。

pilot

【`paɪlət】

n. [C] 駕駛員，飛行員 vt. 駕駛(飛機)

飛機上常見的機組人員(the crew)有：飛行員(pilot)，機長(captain)，跟空服員(flight attendant)。在以前性別意識比較不平等的年代，空少跟空姐會分別稱為：steward 和stewardess。乘客則是passenger。

- crew 【kru】 n. [C] 全體機組人員；全體船員
- captain 【`kæptɪn】 n. [C] 機長；船長
- attendant 【ə`tɛndənt】 n. [C] 服務員；侍者
- steward 【`stjuwɚd】 n. [C] 管家；管事
- passenger 【`pæsndʒɚ】 n. [C] 乘客；旅客

例句

Have you ever seen a female pilot?
你見過女飛行員嗎？

會話

A: What does Jonny do?
強尼是做什麼的？

B: He is a pilot.
他是一位駕駛員。

fasten

【`fæsən】

vt. 紮牢；繫緊

坐上你的機位後，你一定會聽到空服員告訴你務必要繫緊安全帶，繫住安全帶(seat belt)，我們除了fasten這一個字可以用之外，還可以用動詞片語buckle up。

- belt 【bɛlt】 n. [C] 帶子，帶狀物
- buckle 【`bʌk!】 n. [C] 扣帶，扣子；vt., vi. 扣住，扣緊

例句

For the sake of your safety, please fasten your seat belt.
為了您的安全，請繫上您的安全帶。

Buckle up, or you will get fined.
請繫上安全帶，否則您將被罰款。

會話

A: Could you please turn off your cell phone and fasten your seatbelt?
可以請你手機關機然後繫上安全帶嗎？

B: OK.
好的。

baggage

【`bægɪdʒ】
n. [U] 行李

到了機場，首先要做的事就是托運行李(check in)。行李有兩種，可以帶上飛機的叫做手提行李(suitcase或是hand bag)；而需要托運的則是大型的baggage或是luggage。

- suitcase 【`sutəb!】 n. [C] 手提箱
- luggage 【`lʌgɪdʒ】 n. [U] 行李

例句

The traveler checked his baggage again before boarding the plane.
那位旅客在登機前再次地檢查了他的行李。
Where is the baggage room in this train station?
車站裡的行李房在哪？

會話

A: I am missing three suitcases. Please help me find my baggage.
我少了三件行李。請幫我尋找行李。
B: Please fill out the form first.
請先填表格。

claim

【klem】

vt. 認領，索取；自稱，聲稱；主張

下了飛機，當然就要去領行李啦，提領行李區是baggage claim area。此外，claim還有說明跟聲稱的意思。

例句

Fiona claimed her purse at the lost and found.
費歐娜在失物招領區認領了她丟掉的錢包。

Winnie claimed that she lost her luggage.
溫妮聲稱她丟掉了行李。

會話

A: Excuse me, where is the baggage claim area?
對不起，那裡是行李提領區？

B: It's on the second floor.
它在二樓。

declare

【dɪ`klɛr】

vt. 宣佈，宣告；申報(納稅品等)

到了機場的海關(customs)，稽查人員通常會問你有麼有什麼東西是要申報(declare)的。此外，declare也有向大眾宣布自己狀態的意思。

■ customs【`kʌstəmz】n. 海關

例句

America declared its independence in 1776.
美國在1776年宣布獨立。
Kelly had nothing to declare.
凱莉沒有什麼東西要申報的。

會話

A: Do you have anything to declare?
　您有任何東西要申報嗎？
B: I have nothing to declare.
　我沒有東西要申報。

board

【bord】

vt. 上(船，飛機等)

因為登上飛機或是船，我們會用board這一個字，所以boarding pass就是登機證的意思。此外，出境大門上我們會看見Emigration，表示出境；入境則是Immigration。

- emigration 【,ɛmə`greʃən】 n. [U] 移出；出境
- immigration 【,ɪmə`greʃən】 n. [U] 移入；入境

例句

The passengers should board the plane at 10 o'clock.
乘客應在十點登機。

Please bring the boarding pass with you.
請你要帶登機證。

會話

A: May I see your passport and boarding pass, please?
我可以看一下你的護照跟登機證嗎？

B: Sure. Here you are.
好的。在這兒。

transfer

【træns`fɝ】

vt., vi 轉乘(飛機、車)

如果搭乘的不是直航的班機(direct flight)，而是需要轉機的航線(connecting flight)，記得要先找到機場的flight connection counter辦理轉機的程序。

- direct 【də`rɛkt】 vt. 指向；指導；adj. 直接的
- connect 【kə`nɛkt】 vt. 連接；使有關係

例句

Jenny flew to Singapore and then transferred to a plane to London.

珍妮飛往新加坡然後轉機前往倫敦。

You can take a train to the central station and transfer to a shuttle bus.

你可以搭火車去中央車站然後轉乘接駁車。

會話

A: Is this the train to Kaohsiung?

這是去高雄的火車嗎？

B: No. You should take the next train, get off at the next stop, and transfer to the train to Kaohsiung.

不是。你應該要搭下一班火車，在下一站下車。然後轉乘去高雄的火車。

cancel

【`kæns!】

vt. 取消，廢除，刪除

已經預訂(book)的機票，如果要改訂或不搭乘了，記得一定要拿cancellation form(取消退費書)取消你的班機。

■ cancellation【,kænsə`leʃən】n. [U] 取消

例句

If you want to cancel your flight, please call in advance.
如果你想要取消班機，請事先打電話通知。

The fair was cancelled because of the heavy rain.
園遊會因為大雨而取消了。

會話

A: Sorry. The flight to Moscow has been cancelled because of the heavy snow.
抱歉。前往莫斯科的班機因為大雪而取消。

B: What!
什麼！

upgrade

【`ʌp`gred】

vt. 升等、提升

如果你有飛航的VIP卡，或是剛好運氣好，航空公司會幫你座位升等。升等座位還可以說bump you up to the first class。如果你要再確認座位或航班，我們會用reconfirm。

- bump 【bʌmp】 vt., vi. 碰，撞
- reconfirm 【,rikən`fɝm】 vt. 再確認

例句

The airline upgraded Spence when he arrived late and the economy class was full.

當史賓賽遲到且經濟艙已客滿時，航空公司幫他機位升等。

Download the application, and you can upgrade your smart phone to version 4.

下載這一個應用程式，然後你的智慧型手機就會升級成版本4。

會話

A: The airline didn't have any seats in economy class so it bumped me up to business class.

他們經濟艙沒有位子了，所以將我的機位升等為商務艙。

B: That's great.

那真是太好了。

terminal

【`tɝmən!】

n. [C] 航空站；(火車或客運)總站　adj. 終點的

用在空運中，terminal指的是機場的航廈；而在一般的交通英文裡，terminal station就是終點站。目的地我們會說destination。

■ destination【͵dɛstə`neʃən】n. [C] 終點站，目的地

例句

Tina got off the bus at the terminal station.
提娜在終點站下公車。

Passengers to Rome should go to Terminal Two.
要去羅馬的乘客應到第二航廈。

會話

A: I need to go to the International Terminal to catch a connecting flight.
我要去國際航廈搭轉乘飛機。

B: Just take Shuttle Bus 2. Shuttles come about every five minutes.
請搭捷駁車二號。每五分鐘會來一班。

elevator

【`ɛlə͵vetɚ】

n. [C] 電梯

在機場或是車站捷運站，為了運輸的方便，常常會有電梯的設置。一般的電梯稱做elevator，或簡稱lift。電扶梯則稱做escalator。除了電梯、接駁車shuttle bus也是常見的站內或者是站間的運輸工具喔！

- lift 【lɪft】 vt. 提高；n. [C] 電梯
- escalator 【`ɛskə͵letɚ】 n. [C] 電扶梯
- shuttle 【`ʃʌtl̩】 vt. 穿梭；n. [C] 梭子；短程穿梭

例句

Many airports have both elevators and escalators.
很多機場都有電梯跟電扶梯。

Tom took a lift to the tenth floor.
湯姆搭電梯到10樓。

會話

A: How can I get to the cafeteria in the hotel?
怎麼到飯店餐廳？

B: Take the elevator to the second floor. Turn right when you get off the elevator.
搭電梯到二樓，出電梯後右轉。

sick

【sɪk】

adj. 不舒服，生病的

生病我們會說get sick；身體感覺不舒服是feel ill或是feel uncomfortable。身體感覺不錯，我們會說feel well。

- ill 【ɪl】 adj. 不舒服
- uncomfortable 【ʌn`kʌmfɚtəb!】 adj. 不舒適的
- well 【wɛl】 adj. (身體感覺)好的，健康的

例句

After walking in the rain for an hour, Emily felt a little sick.

在雨中行走了一個小時之後，愛蜜莉覺得有些不舒服。

Little Tony was sick with influenza.

小湯米生病感冒了。

會話

A: You look terrible! What's the matter?

你氣色看起來很糟！你怎麼了？

B: I feel very sick now.

我現在覺得很不舒服。

healthy

【`hɛlθɪ】

adj. 健康的，健全的

身體健康是health。健全其他的說法還有sound跟well。不健康是unhealthy，而虛弱是weak。

- health 【`hɛlθ】 n. [U] 健康
- sound 【saʊnd】 adj. 健全的；n. [C] [U] 聲音
- weak 【wik】 adj. 虛弱的

例句

Regular exercise can keep you healthy.
規律的運動可以保持你健康。
The economic situation of this society is not healthy.
這個社會的經濟狀況並不健全。

會話

A: Did you quit smoking?
你戒菸了？
B: Yes, because I want to get healthy.
是啊，因為我想保持健康。

cold

【kold】

adj. 冷的；寒冷的　n. [C] 感冒

天氣變涼轉冷，我們會說It is cold.。而cold另一個意思是感冒，流行性感冒叫flu。catch a cold就是染上感冒，也可以說成come down with a cold。

■ flu【flu】n. [C] 流行性感冒(influenza)

例句

It is cold in winter.
冬天很冷

Mike caught a cold and took sick leave.
麥可感冒，然後請了病假。

會話

A: It is cold.
好冷喔。

B: Put on a coat, or you will catch a cold.
穿上外套，否則你會感冒的。

disease

【dɪˋziz】

n. [C] 病，疾病

生病了，我們會說get a disease。疾病還可以說illness跟sickness。心臟病是heart disease，肺病是lung disease。生病要請病假則是take a sick leave。

- illness 【ˋɪlnɪs】 n. [C] [U] 疾病
- sickness 【ˋsɪknɪs】 n. [C] [U] 疾病
- leave 【liv】 n. 休假；vi. 離開

例句

Lung cancer is a deadly disease.
肺癌是一個致命的疾病。
Helen became ill with a disease.
海倫因病而身體不適。

會話

A: Do you have any heart disease?
你有心臟方面的疾病嗎？
B: No.
沒有。

physical

【`fɪzɪk!】
adj. 身體的，肉體的

學校的P.E. class(體育課)的全名就是physical education class。physical check-up就是身體檢查。physical disease則是生理上的疾病。心理上的是mental，心靈上上的是spiritual。

- mental 【`mɛnt!】 adj. 心理上的，精神上的
- spiritual 【`spɪrɪtʃʊəl】 adj. 心靈上的，靈性的

例句

Penny is going to have a physical examination.
潘妮將要接受身體檢查。
Pitt dislikes P.E. class in school.
彼特不喜歡學校的體育課。

會話

A: Which subject do you like in school?
你喜歡學校裡的哪一個科目？
B: Physical Education.
體育。

pain

【pen】

n. [C] [U] 疼痛，痛苦 vt., vi. 使疼痛

當有wound(傷口)或是scar(傷痕)時，我們就會感受到疼痛。要注意的是"No pains, no gains"(不勞則無獲)裡的pains是「努力」的意思。

- wound 【wund】 n. [C] 傷口
- scar 【skar】 n. [C] 傷疤，傷痕

例句

I have a pain in my stomach.
我胃痛。
Do you have pain anywhere else?
你其他地方還會痛嗎？

會話

A: I have a sharp pain in my stomach. Can you help get the medicine for me?
我胃部劇痛，可以請你幫我拿藥嗎？
B: Sure. Where did you put it?
好的，你放在哪兒？

hurt

【hɝt】

vt. 傷害 vi. 痛 adj. 疼痛的

心痛或頭痛是ache，痠痛或是喉嚨痛是sore。要注意hurt是不規則變化的動詞：hurt-hurt-hurt。

- ache 【ek】 vt. 疼痛；n. [C] [U] 疼痛
- sore 【sor】 adj. 痠痛的；n. [C] 痛處

例句

The stone hurt my foot.
那個石頭傷了我的腳。

My arm hurts.
我的腳好痛。

會話

A: Does it hurt?
會痛嗎？

B: Yes. I feel dizzy, and my neck hurts all the time.
會啊。我覺得頭昏，而且我脖子也一直痛。

doctor

【`daktɚ】
n. [C] 醫生

醫院裡的醫護人員(medics)，主要是有醫生跟護士(nurse)。醫生又有內科醫生(surgeon)跟外科醫生(physician)之分。病人是patient。

- nurse 【nɝs】 n. [C] 護士
- surgeon 【`sɝdʒən】 n. [C] 內科醫生
- physician 【fɪ`zɪʃən】 n. [C] 外科醫生
- patient 【`peʃənt】 n. [C] 病人

例句

You look ill. I think you should go to see a doctor.
你看起來不太好。我想你應該去看醫生。

會話

A: What does Jeff's son do?
傑夫兒子的職業是什麼？

B: He is an ear, nose, and throat doctor.
他是一位耳喉鼻科醫生。

diagnose

【`daɪəgnoz】
vt. 診斷

去看醫生，醫生先會觀察(observe)你的狀況，在做診斷。診斷書就是diagnosis。觀察室是observation room。

- diagnosis 【,daɪəg`nosɪs】 n. [C] [U] 診斷，診斷書
- observe 【əb`zɝv】 vt. 觀察
- observation 【,ɑbzɝ`veʃən】 n. [C] [U] 觀察，觀察力

例句

The doctor diagnosed Jimmy's disease as a rare disease.
醫生診斷吉米罹患罕見疾病。

The Lins remained silent until the surgeon told them the diagnosis of their mother's condition.
林家人持續沉默不語，直到醫生告訴他們其母親的病況。

會話

A: Have you ever heard from Helen?
你有聽說Helen的消息嗎？

B: Yes, and she was diagnosed with lung cancer last month.
有啊，她上個月被診斷出有肺癌。

cure

【kjʊr】

vt. 治療 n. [C] [U] 治療

治療疾病除了cure，還有treat以及heal。而治療法則是cure，treatment以及remedy。

- treat 【trit】 vt. 對待；治療
- heal 【hil】 vt. 治癒；治療
- remedy 【`rɛmədɪ】 n. [C] [U] 治療法
- treatment 【`tritmənt】 n. [C] [U] 治療法

例句

The doctor cured Greg of his headache.
醫生治療葛瑞格的頭痛。

會話

A: Here is the prescription for you. I'm sure the medicine will cure your sore threat.
這是你的處方籤，我相信這些藥可以治好你的喉嚨痛。

B: Thank you.
謝謝。

medicine

【`mɛdəsn】
n. [U] 藥物

治療法有很多種，其中一種就是吃藥。藥還可以說drug，藥丸是pill，而止痛劑是painkiller。開藥是prescribe，處方籤是prescription。

- drug【drʌg】n. [C] 藥
- pill【pɪl】n. [C] 藥丸，藥片
- painkiller【`pen,kɪlɚ】n. [C] 止痛劑
- prescribe【prɪ`skraɪb】vt., vi. 開(藥方)，為…開(藥方)
- prescription【prɪ`skrɪpʃən】n. [C] 處方，藥方

例句

Take the medicine after each meal.
飯後服藥。

會話

A: What can I do for you?
您需要什麼嗎？
B: I need some medicine for my flu.
我需要一些感冒藥。

pharmacy

【`farməsɪ】

n. [C] 藥房

拿藥要去藥局，藥局還可以說drug store或是the pharmacist's。而醫院是hospital，診所則是clinic。

- pharmacist 【`farməsɪst】 n. [C] 藥劑師
- hospital 【`hospɪt!】 n. [C] [U] 醫院
- clinic 【`klɪnɪk】 n. [C] [U] 診所

例句

There is a pharmacy around the street corner.
街角有一間藥房。

Please have the prescription filled at the pharmacy.
請去藥房抓藥。

會話

A: Where is the pharmacy?
藥房在哪兒？

B: It is next to the hospital.
它就在醫院旁邊。

surgery

【`sɝdʒərɪ】
n. [U] 手術

手術也是一種治療法。接受手術叫做have a surgery；而動手術是perform a surgery。手術其他的說法是operation跟procedure。

- operation 【,ɑpə`reʃən】 n. [C] [U] 操作；手術
- procedure 【prə`sidʒɚ】 n. [C] [U] 程序；手術

例句

The patient needs surgery.
這個病人需要動手術。

The doctor performed an operation on the ill patient.
醫生對這位病人動手術。

會話

A: She looks fake.
她看起來好假。

B: She may have had plastic surgery.
她可能動過整型手術吧。

emergency

【ɪ`mɝdʒənsɪ】

n. [C] 緊急的事情

醫院裡面的ER指的就是急救室“emergency room”。在急救室裡，常常有需要急救的病人，急救就是first aid。此外，一旦有緊急的事發生，保險(insurance)就是一件很重要的事情了。

- first aid 【`fɝst`ed】 n. 急救
- insurance 【ɪn`ʃʊrəns】 n. [U] 保險；保險金額

例句

If there is a fire or any emergency, call 911.
要是有火災或是任何緊急的事情，撥119。
You can prepare a first-aid kit when you go camping.
當你要去露營時，你可以準備一個急救箱。

會話

A: Could you tell me someone we can contact in case of emergency?
請告訴我們你的警急聯絡人？
B: OK. You can contact my mother.
嗯，你可以連絡我母親

price

【praɪs】

n. [C] 價格，價錢　vt. 給…定價；給…標價

購物時，物件的價格常常會影響人們是否購買。在price tag（標籤吊牌）上我們就可以看到價錢，我們還可以問店員，這個價錢是否是tax-free（免稅）還是tax included（含稅）的價錢。

- tag【tæg】n. [C] 標籤
- tax【tæks】n. [C] [U] 稅金

例句

William bought a house at a high price.
威廉以高價買了一間房子。

The washing machine is priced at 6,000 NT dollars.
這台洗衣機標價6, 000元台幣。

會話

A: Can I get a refund if I remove a price tag?
要是我把標籤吊牌拿下來了，我還可以退換貨嗎？

B: Sorry. I am afraid you can't.
抱歉，恐怕不行。

pay

【pe】

vt. 支付；付款給 n. [C] 薪俸；報酬

價錢沒問題，就要去櫃檯(counter)付帳。付錢我們一般都是說 pay the money。而不同的是在餐廳或是飯店付帳，我們會說 check the bill。

- counter 【`kaʊntɚ】 n. [C] 櫃台
- check 【tʃɛk】 vt. 檢查
- bill 【bɪl】 n. [C] 帳單

例句

Roy paid a very high price for the diamond necklace.
羅伊以很高的價錢買得這一條鑽石項鍊。

Jenny negotiated with her boss for higher pay.
珍妮跟他老闆協商加薪。

會話

A: Can I pay for the bill by credit card?
我可以用信用卡付款嗎？

B: Of course.
當然可以。

cost

【kɔst】

vt. 花費　n. [C] 成本

我們付錢購物，會用pay或是spend money來表示。然而。商品花費我們多少錢，我們則會用cost這一個動詞。此外，cost也有成本的意思，所以低價(成本)航空就叫作low cost airline。

■ spend【spɛnd】vt. 花(錢，時間)，花費

動詞變化：spend-spent-spent

例句

That smart phone cost Jerry 30, 000 dollars.

這一支智慧型手機花了傑瑞三萬元。

Many manufacturers now are trying to reduce production cost.

許多製造商現在試圖要降低生產成本。

對話

A: How much does this laptop cost?

這一台筆記型電腦要多少錢？

B: It cost me thirty thousand dollars.

它花了我三萬元。

bargain

【`bargɪn】

vi. 討價還價 n [C] 特價商品，便宜貨

在夜市(night market)或攤販(stand)要付帳時，難免討價還價。討價還價就是用bargain這一個字。但是網路拍賣購物的出價，則是用bid這一個字。

■ market 【`markɪt】 n. [C] 市場，市集
■ stand 【stænd】 n. [C] 小攤販
■ bid 【bɪd】 vt. (拍賣)出價，喊價

例句

In a night market, you can bargain with vendors.
在夜市，你可以跟小販討價還價。
This laptop is a real bargain at such a low price.
這台筆記型電腦真是特價商品。

會話

A: Can you lower the price for me?
你可以降價嗎？
B: Sorry, but no bargaining here.
抱歉，但是這兒不二價。

lower

【`loɚ】

vt. 降低

無論是討價還價，或是ask for a discount(打折)，都是希望賣家可以降低商品價錢，讓商品便宜(cheap)一些。降低價格就是lower the price。

- discount 【`dɪskaʊnt】 n. [C] 折扣；vt., vi. 打折
- cheap 【tʃip】 adj. 便宜的，低廉的

例句

Can you lower the price a little bit, please?

可以請你降價一些嗎？

We have lowered our living expenses since the prices of goods are rising.

自從物價上漲之後，我們降低了生活開支。

會話

A: Would it be possible for you to lower the price a little?

你可以降價一些嗎？

B: Well, I can give you a ten percent discount.

呃，我可以給你打九折。

sale

【sel】

n. [U] 賣，出售；營業，推銷

for sale意思是出售，所以not for sale指的就是非賣品。而on sale指的就是拍賣的，而garage sale指的就是二手拍賣會。百貨公司周年慶則會用anniversary來表示。

- garage【gə`rɑʒ】n. [C] 車房，車庫
- anniversary【,ænə`vɝsərɪ】n. [C] 周年紀念，周年紀念日

例句

Every item in this shop is on sale.
這件店裡的每件商品正在拍賣中。

The salesperson worked day and night to sell more products.
銷售員日以繼夜地工作以賣出更多的產品。

會話

A: Are you going to the yard sale with us?
你要跟我們一起去二手拍賣會嗎？

B: No, thanks.
不用了，謝謝你。

cash

【kæʃ】

n. [U] 現金，現款　vt. 兌現(支票)

出國旅行，許多人會帶些現款在身上。紙幣是bill，而零錢是change。而dollar除了有「元」的意思之外，還有全球通用的「美金」之意。

- bill 【bɪl】 n. [C] 紙幣
- dollar 【`dɑlɚ】 n. [C] 元；美金
- coin 【kɔɪn】 n. [C] 硬幣；錢幣

例句

Are you paying in cash or by credit card?

你要用現金付款還是用信用卡？

Could you cash this check for me?

可以請你幫我兌現這張支票嗎？

會話

A: I am out of cash. Can you lend me some money?

我身上沒現金。你可以借我些錢嗎？

B: Well, how much do you need?

呃，你需要多少？

check

【tʃɛk】

n. [C] 支票

出國旅遊購物，付款除了現金之外，還可以用旅行支票(traveler's check)支付。此外，塑膠貨幣像是信用卡(credit card)或是現金卡(debit card)也是常見的付款選擇。支票還可以寫成cheque。

- traveller【`trævlɚ】n. [C] 旅行者
- credit card n. [C] 信用卡
- debit card n. [C] 現金卡

例句

Can I pay for this by check?
我可以用支票付款嗎？
Sorry, but we cannot honor the check.
抱歉，但我們不能對兌現這支票。

會話

A: Where can I cash a traveler's check?
我可以去哪兒兌換旅行支票？
B: Please go to the fourth window.
請到二號窗口。

service

【`sɝvɪs】

n. [U] 服務

售後服務就是service這一個字。客戶服務就是customer service，送貨服務是delivery service，而飯店客房服務是room service。不同的是，退換貨服務叫作refund。

- delivery 【dɪ`lɪvərɪ】 n. [U] 傳遞，傳送
- refund 【rɪ`fʌnd】 vt. 退還；n. [U] 退還

例句

The room service in this hotel is good.
這間旅社的客房服務很棒。

This company is famous for its customer service.
這間公司以它的客戶服務聞名。

會話

A: Hello, Holiday Inn. How may I help you?
嗨，假日旅店。需要什麼呢？

B: This is Room 808, and I need room service.
這裡是808房，我需要客房服務。

shop

【ʃap】

n. [C] 商店，零售店 vt. 購物，逛商店

除了shop，我們還有購物中心mall，以及暢貨中心outlet。去購物我們會說go shopping。店員也可以說shopping assistant。shopaholic是購物狂的意思。

- mall 【mɔl】 n. [C] 購物中心
- outlet 【`aʊt,lɛt】 n. [C] 銷路，商行
- assistant 【ə`sɪstənt】 n. [C] 協助者，助手，助理

例句

My sister works in a flower shop.
我姐在花店工作。

Jean went shopping last week.
琴上周去購物。

會話

A: Do you shop online often?
你常上網購物嗎？

B: Yes, and I think shopping online is very convenient.
是啊，而且我覺得上網購物很方便。

store

【stor】

n. [C] 店　vt. 存放

store跟其他字結合，就會形成不同的字，例如department store（百貨公司），convenience store（便利商店），或是stationery store（文具店）。store跟shop都是商店之意，在英式英文裡，store趨向於大型的商店，如百貨公司。

- department 【dɪ`partmənt】 n. [C] 部門
- convenient 【kən`vinjənt】 adj. [U] 方便，舒適
- stationery 【`steʃən,ɛrɪ】 n. [U] 文具，信紙

例句

There are many convenience stores in Taiwan.
台灣有很多便利商店。

Ants store food for the winter.
螞蟻存食物以過冬。

會話

A: Where shall we meet?
　我們要在哪兒見面？

B: How about the café in that bookstore?
　書店裡的咖啡店如何？

clerk

【klɝk】

n. [C] 店員

百貨公司或是服飾店裡的員工，我們可以稱呼他們clerk。餐廳的服務生則是server或是waiter。

■ server【`sɝvɚ】n. [C] 服務生，侍者

例句

Lillian got a job as a hotel clerk.
麗麗安在飯店當店員。
The clerk introduced dresses to Maria.
這個店員介紹洋裝給瑪利亞。

會話

A: Can I get a map of this town?
我可以要一份這城鎮的地圖嗎？
B: I am sure the desk clerk can help you with that.
我想櫃台服務生可以幫你忙。

customer

【`kʌstəmɚ】
n. [C] 顧客；客人

來店裡光顧的客人除了可以用customer表示之外，我們還可以說consumer(消費者)，buyer(買者)，或者是client (顧客)

- consumer 【kən`sjumɚ】 n. [C] 消費者
- buyer 【`baɪɚ】 n. [C] 買者
- client 【`klaɪənt】 n. [C] 顧客，客戶

例句

The customer is always right.
顧客永遠是對的。
It is getting harder to deal with customer complaints.
處裡客訴這件事越來越難了。

會話

A: Do you like that department store?
你喜歡那家百貨公司嗎？
B: No. Customer service there is quite poor.
不喜歡，那 的客服很差。

單字附錄

本單字附錄摘取最基本最常用單詞，並依主題分類，讓您好查、好記、又好背。

人稱

人稱		主格 (subject)	所有格 (possessive)	受格 (object)
第一人稱	我	I	my	me
	我們	we	our	us
第二人稱	你	you	your	you
	你們	you	your	you
第三人稱	他	he	his	him
	她	she	her	her
	它	it	its	it
	她/他/它們	they	their	them

人稱代名詞(pronouns)

人稱		所有格代名詞	反身代名詞
第一人稱	我的	mine	myself
	我們的	ours	ourselves
第二人稱	你的	yours	yourself
	你們的	yours	yourselves
第三人稱	他的	his	himself
	她的	hers	herself
	它的	its	itself
	她/他/它們的	theirs	themselves

冠詞(articles)

冠詞	單數	複數
不定	a /an	×
	the	the
限定	this	these
	that	those

人物 people

嬰兒	baby, infant
小孩	child, kid
青少年	teenager
年輕人	youth
成人	adult, grown-up
老人	the elderly
男孩	boy
女孩	girl
男人	man
女人	woman
男的；雄性的	male
女的；雌性的	female
先生	Mister
紳士	gentleman
小姐	Miss
太太	Mistress
人(單數)	person, human, guy
人(複數)	people

人體 human body

頭	head
額頭	forehead
眉毛	eyebrow
眼睛	eye
睫毛	eyelash
鼻子	nose
頰	cheek
嘴巴	mouth
嘴唇	lip
牙齒	teeth
下巴	chin
頭髮	hair
鬍子	beard
頸	neck
肩膀	shoulder
手臂	arm
手肘	elbow
手腕	wrist
手	hand
手指	finger
手掌	palm
指甲	nail
胸	chest
腹	belly
腰	waist
臀	hip
背部	back
大腿	thigh

膝蓋	knee
腿	leg
腳踝	ankle
腳	foot (複數是feet)
腳趾	toe
皮膚	skin

家人親屬 family and relatives

父親	father
母親	mother
繼父	step-father
繼母	step-mother
養父	adopted father
養母	adopted mother
家長(常用複數)	parents
兒子	son
女兒	daughter
繼子	step son
繼女	step daughter
養子	adopted son
養女	adopted daughter
兄弟	brother
姊妹	sister
手足	siblings (慣用複數)
小孩	child, kid
堂表兄弟姊妹	cousin
丈夫	husband
太太	wife

夫妻	couple
祖父、外公	grandfather
祖母、外婆	grandmother
曾祖父	great grandfather
曾祖母	great grandmother
外/孫子	grandson
外/孫女	granddaughter
曾孫子	great grandson
曾孫女	great granddaughter
公公、岳父	father-in-law
婆婆、岳母	mother-in-law
女婿	son-in-law
媳婦	daughter-in-law
伯伯、叔叔、舅舅	uncle
伯母、嬸嬸、舅母、阿姨	aunt
外甥、姪子	nephew
外甥女、姪女	nlece
姊夫、妹夫、連襟	brother-in-law
嫂嫂、弟媳、妯娌	sister-in-law

時間 time

時間	time
今天	today
今晚	tonight
昨天	yesterday
明天	tomorrow
前天	the day before yesterday
後天	the day after tomorrow

前幾天	the other day
清晨	dawn
早晨	morning
白天	day
中午	noon
下午	afternoon
傍晚	evening
夜晚	night
午夜	midnight
過去	past
現在	now, present
未來	future
小時	hour
分鐘	minute
秒	second
片刻	moment

星期 week

星期一	Monday
星期二	Tuesday
星期三	Wednesday
星期四	Thursday
星期五	Friday
星期六	Saturday
星期日	Sunday

月份 months

一月	January
二月	February
三月	March
四月	April
五月	May
六月	June
七月	July
八月	August
九月	September
十月	October
十一月	November
十二月	December

季節 seasons

春	spring
夏	summer
秋	fall, autumn
冬	winter

數字 numbers／基數

一	one
二	two

三	three
四	four
五	five
六	six
七	seven
八	eight
九	nine
十	ten
十一	eleven
十二	twelve
十三	thirteen
十四	fourteen
十五	fifteen
十六	sixteen
十七	seventeen
十八	eighteen
十九	nineteen
二十	twenty
三十	thirty
四十	forty
五十	fifty
六十	sixty
七十	seventy
八十	eighty
百	hundred
千	thousand
萬	ten thousand
百萬	million
十億	billion

數字 numbers／序數

第一	first
第二	second
第三	third
第四	fourth
第五	fifth
第六	sixth
第七	seventh
第八	eighth
第九	ninth
第十	tenth
第十一	eleventh
第十二	twelfth
第十三	thirteenth
第十四	fourteenth
第十五	fifteenth
第十六	sixteenth
第十七	seventeenth
第十八	eighteenth
第十九	nineteenth
第二十	twentieth
第二十一	twenty first
第二十二	twenty second
第二十三	twenty third
第二十四	twenty fourth
第二十五	twenty fifth
第三十	thirtieth
第四十	fortieth
第五十	fiftieth

第六十	sixtieth
第七十	seventieth
第八十	eightieth
第一百	hundredth
第一千	thousandth
第一萬	one thousandth
第百萬	millionth
第十億	billionth

國家名稱 nationality

亞洲	Asia
亞洲人	Asian
歐洲	Europe
歐洲人	European
非洲	Africa
非洲人	African
澳洲	Australia
澳洲人	Australian
中國	China
中國人	Chinese
台灣	Taiwan
台灣人	Taiwanese
日本	Japan
日本人	Japanese
韓國	Korea
韓國人	Korean
越南	Vietnam
越南人	Vietnamese

泰國	Thailand
泰國人	Thai
菲律賓	the Philippines
菲律賓人	Filipino
新加坡	Singapore
新加坡人	Singaporean
馬來西亞	Malaysia
馬來西亞人	Malaysian
英國	England
英國人	British
法國	France
法國人	French
德國	Germany
德國人	German
西班牙	Spain
西班牙人	Spanish
葡萄牙	Portugal
葡萄牙人	Portuguese
義大利	Italy
義大利人	Italian
希臘	Greece
希臘人	Greek
俄羅斯	Russia
俄羅斯人	Russian
歐盟	the European Union
美國	America
美國人	American
加拿大	Canada
加拿大人	Canadian
巴西	Brazil
巴西人	Brazilian

南非	South Africa
南非人	South African
埃及	Egypt
埃及人	Egyptian
阿拉伯	Arabia
阿拉伯人	Arab, Arabian
印度	India
印度人	Indian

單位 measurement units

公分	centimeter
公尺	meter
公里	kilometer
英吋	inch
英呎	foot
英哩	mile
英碼	yard
公克	gram
公斤	kilogram
磅	pound
公升	liter
攝氏	Celsius, Centigrade
華氏	Fahrenheit
一度	degree
一打	dozen

星座 star signs

牡羊座	Aries
金牛座	Taurus
雙子座	Gemini
巨蟹座	Cancer
獅子座	Leo
處女座	Virgo
天秤座	Libra
天蠍座	Scorpio
射手座	Sagittarius
魔羯座	Capricorn
水瓶座	Aquarius
雙魚座	Pieces

生肖 Chinese zodiac signs

鼠	mouse
牛	ox
虎	tiger
兔	rabbit
龍	dragon
蛇	snake
馬	horse
羊	goat
猴	monkey
雞	rooster
狗	dog
豬	pig

常見職業 occupations

學生	student
教師	teacher
勞工	laborer, worker
技師	technician
工程師	engineer
業務員	salesperson
公務員	civil servant
警察	police officer
消防員	fire fighter
律師	lawyer
從政人員	politician
農夫	farmer
漁夫	fisherman
商人	businessperson
司機	driver
醫生	doctor
牙醫	dentist
護士	nurse
作家	writer
記者	reporter
畫家	painter
舞者	dancer
藝術家	artist
建築師	architect
設計師	designer
歌手	singer
演員	actor/actress
理髮師	hairdresser

美容師	cosmetologist
導遊	tour guide
廚師	cook, chef
麵包師傅	backer
助理	assistant
秘書	secretary
保母	babysitter
軍人	soldier
企業家	entrepreneur
科學家	scientist
自由業者	freelancer
白領階級	white-collar
藍領階級	blue-collar
家庭主婦	housewife
失業者	unemployed

情緒形容詞 emotions

快樂的	happy
喜悅的	joyful
歡樂的	cheerful
興奮的	excited
憤怒的	angry
發狂的	mad
無聊的	bored
傷心的	sad
憂鬱的	depressed
挫折的	upset
抑鬱的	gloomy

煩惱的	troubled
焦慮的	anxious
擔心的	worried
害怕的	afraid
樂觀的	optimistic
積極的	active
悲觀的	pessimistic
消極的	passive

顏色 colors

紅色	red
粉紅色	pink
橙色	orange
黃色	yellow
金色	golden
銀色	silver
綠色	green
藍色	blue
靛色	indigo
紫色	purple
咖啡色	brown
棕色	brunette
黑色	black
白色	white
米色	beige
灰色	gray
深色	dark
淺色	light
透明無色	transparent

方位 directions

前	front
後	back
上	up
下	down
左	left
右	right
東	east
西	west
南	south
北	north
東北	northeast
東南	southeast
西北	northwest
西南	southcast
這裡	here
那裡	there
對面的	opposite
在…旁邊	beside
附近	nearby

食物 food／基本單字 basics

早餐	breakfast
早午餐	brunch
午餐	lunch
晚餐，正餐	dinner, supper

湯	soup
沙拉	salad
食物	food
飲食，食物	diet
一餐，一頓飯	meal
一份	serving, helping
碟，盤；一盤菜，菜餚	dish

食物 food／穀物 grains，主食 staple food

米	rice
麥	wheat
馬鈴薯	potato
麵(常複數)	noodles
義大利麵條	spaghetti
義大利麵	pasta
玉米	corn
麥片	cereal
餃子	dumpling

食物 food／麵包類 bakery

比薩	pizza
漢堡	hamburger
三明治	sandwich
吐司	toast
派	pie

麵包	bread
小圓麵包，小圓糕點	bun
煎餅	pancake

食物 food／肉類 meat

牛肉	beef
牛排	steak
雞肉	chicken
火雞	turkey
豬肉	pork
鴨肉	duck
鵝肉	goose
羊肉	lamb
火腿	ham
培根	bacon
香腸	sausage
魚	fish
蝦	shrimp, pawn
龍蝦	lobster
海鮮	seafood

食物 food／蔬菜類 vegetables

洋蔥	onion
蒜	garlic
薑	ginger

包心菜	cabbage
萵苣	lettuce
菠菜	spinach
蘑菇	mushroom
胡蘿蔔	carrot
南瓜	pumpkin
地瓜	yam
黃瓜	cucumber
豌豆	pea
豆	bean
核果	nut
花生	peanut
大豆	soybean
豆腐	tofu

食物 food／水果類 fruits

蘋果	apple
柳橙	orange
橘子	tangerine
檸檬	lemon
桃子	peach
梨	pear
草莓	strawberry
莓	berry
櫻桃	cherry
梅子	plum
荔枝	lychee
葡萄	grape

葡萄柚	grapefruit
香蕉	banana
木瓜	papaya
鳳梨	pineapple
芭樂	guava
芒果	mango
番茄	tomato
椰子	coconut
瓜，甜瓜	melon
西瓜	watermelon

食物 food／甜點 dessert，零食 snack

甜甜圈	doughnut, donut
餅乾	cookie, biscuit
洋芋片	chip
蛋糕	cake
布朗尼(巧克力小方塊蛋糕)	brownie
布丁	pudding
果凍	jelly
糖果	candy
葡萄乾	raisin
巧克力	chocolate
爆米花	popcorn

食物 food／飲料 drinks and beverages

含酒精飲料	alcohol
啤酒	beer
(烈)酒	liquor
葡萄酒	wine
雞尾酒	cocktail
咖啡	coffee
茶	tea
可樂	coke
汽水	soda
果汁	juice
檸檬汁	lemonade

食物 food／乳製品 dairy products

奶油	butter
乳酪，起司	cheese
蛋	egg
牛奶	milk
優格	yogurt

食物 food／調味類 seasonings

果醬	jam
調味番茄醬	ketchup
醬油	soy-sauce
醋	vinegar
油	oil
糖	sugar
鹽	salt
胡椒粉	pepper

味道 taste

酸的	sour
甜的	sweet
苦的	bitter
鹹的	salty
辣的	spicy, hot
新鮮的	fresh
油膩的	greasy
清淡的	light
好吃的	delicious, yummy
難吃的	yuck
噁心的	disgusting

交通工具 transportation

腳踏車	bicycle, bike
三輪車	tricycle

摩托車	motorcycle
汽車	car
跑車	sports car
箱型車	van
休旅車	recreational vehicle
吉普車	jeep
卡車	truck
貨車	wagon
拖車	trailer
救護車	ambulance
消防車	fire truck
公車	bus
客運	coach
雙層巴士	double-deck bus
小型巴士	minibus
接駁車	shuttle bus
計程車	taxi, cab
火車	train
地下鐵	subway, underground
捷運	Mass Rapid Transit
高鐵	high-speed rail
船	boat
木筏	raft
獨木舟	canoe
渡輪	ferry
遊艇	yacht
貨輪	cargo ship, steamer
潛水艇	submarine
飛機	airplane

公共場所 public places

學校	school
公園	park
動物園	zoo
咖啡廳	café
餐廳	restaurant
熟食店	deli
自助餐廳	cafeteria
旅館	hotel
廁所	toilet
男廁	men's room
女廁	women's room
便利商店	convenient store
超級市場	supermarket
百貨公司	department store
購物中心	shopping mall
免稅商店	duty-free shop
書店	bookstore
市場	market
商店	store, shop
雜貨店	grocery store
夜市	night market
賭場	casino
電影院	movie theater
遊樂園	amusement park
體育館	stadium
健身場	gymnasium
游泳池	swimming pool
警局	police station

郵局	post office
市政廳	city hall
旅客資訊中心	information center
辦公處	office
銀行	bank
法院	court
大學	university
醫院	hospital
藥局	pharmacy, drugstore
廟宇	temple
教堂	church
博物館	museum
畫廊	galley
文化中心	culture center
火車站	train station
公車站	bus stop
加油站	gas station
停車場	parking lot, car park
機場	airport

國際節慶 holidays

新年(一月一日)	New Year's Day
情人節(二月十四日)	Valentine's Day
嘉年華(巴西，二月下旬)	Carnival
婦女節(三月八日)	Women's Day
愚人節(四月一日)	Fool's Day
復活節(春分月圓後第一個星期日)	Easter
勞動節(五月一日)	Labor Day

母親節（五月的第二個禮拜日）	Mother's Day
兒童節（六月一日）	Children's Day
父親節（六月第三個禮拜日）	Father's Day
教師節（台灣九月二十八日）	Teacher's Day
萬聖節（十月三十一日）	Halloween
感恩節（美國十一月最後的禮拜四）	Thanksgiving Day
聖誕節（十二月二十五日）	Christmas
元宵節	Lantern Festival
清明節	Tomb Sweeping Festival
端午節	Dragon Boat Festival
中秋節	Moon Festival
寒假	winter vacation
春假	spring holidays
暑假	summer vacation

不規則動詞變化附錄

本單元依照語言中心公布全民英檢單字表，摘錄最常用的不規則動詞變化，以下單字表依照字母順序排列。

是	現在式 be (am, is, are) 過去式 was, were 過去分詞 been
承受，生產	現在式 bear 過去式 bore 過去分詞 borne, born
打，擊敗，跳動	現在式 beat 過去式 beat 過去分詞 beaten
成為，變成	現在式 become 過去式 became 過去分詞 become
開始，展開	現在式 begin 過去式 began 過去分詞 begun
彎曲，折彎	現在式 bend 過去式 bent 過去分詞 bent

打賭，下賭注	現在式 bet 過去式 bet 過去分詞 bet
咬，叮咬	現在式 bite 過去式 bit 過去分詞 bitten
吹	現在式 blow 過去式 blew 過去分詞 blown
打斷，毀壞	現在式 break 過去式 broke 過去分詞 broken
帶來，拿來	現在式 bring 過去式 brought 過去分詞 brought
廣播，播報	現在式 broadcast 過去式 broadcast 過去分詞 broadcast
建造	現在式 build 過去式 built 過去分詞 built

中文	現在式	過去式	過去分詞
燃燒，灼傷	burn	burned, burnt	burned, burnt
爆炸，破裂	burst	burst	burst
買	buy	bought	bought
能夠，可能	can	could	
捕捉，抓住	catch	caught	caught
選擇	choose	chose	chosen
來	come	came	come

花費，耗費	現在式	cost
	過去式	cost
	過去分詞	cost
剪斷，切，割	現在式	cut
	過去式	cut
	過去分詞	cut
處理，對付，交易	現在式	deal
	過去式	dealt
	過去分詞	dealt
挖掘，發掘	現在式	dig
	過去式	dug
	過去分詞	dug
做	現在式	do (does)
	過去式	did
	過去分詞	done
拉，吸引，畫畫	現在式	draw
	過去式	drew
	過去分詞	drawn
夢，夢想	現在式	dream
	過去式	dreamed, dreamt
	過去分詞	dreamed, dreamt

喝，喝酒	現在式	drink
	過去式	drank
	過去分詞	drunk
開車，驅使	現在式	drive
	過去式	drove
	過去分詞	driven
吃	現在式	eat
	過去式	ate
	過去分詞	eaten
掉落，跌倒	現在式	fall
	過去式	fell
	過去分詞	fallen
餵，飼養	現在式	feed
	過去式	fed
	過去分詞	fed
感覺，觸摸	現在式	feel
	過去式	felt
	過去分詞	felt
爭鬥，打架	現在式	fight
	過去式	fought
	過去分詞	fought

尋找，發現	現在式	find
	過去式	found
	過去分詞	found
飛，消逝	現在式	fly
	過去式	flew
	過去分詞	flown
忘記	現在式	forget
	過去式	forgot
	過去分詞	forgotten
原諒，寬恕	現在式	forgive
	過去式	forgave
	過去分詞	forgiven
冰凍，冷凍	現在式	freeze
	過去式	froze
	過去分詞	frozen
得到，獲得	現在式	get
	過去式	got
	過去分詞	got, gotten
給予，供給	現在式	give
	過去式	gave
	過去分詞	given

去	現在式	go
	過去式	went
	過去分詞	gone
成長，種植	現在式	grow
	過去式	grew
	過去分詞	grown
吊，掛	現在式	hang
	過去式	hung, hanged
	過去分詞	hung, hanged
有	現在式	have (has)
	過去式	had
	過去分詞	had
聽，聽說	現在式	hear
	過去式	heard
	過去分詞	heard
隱藏，躲藏	現在式	hide
	過去式	hid
	過去分詞	hidden, hid
打擊，撞擊	現在式	hit
	過去式	hit
	過去分詞	hit

抱，握，拿著	現在式	hold
	過去式	held
	過去分詞	held
傷害，使疼痛	現在式	hurt
	過去式	hurt
	過去分詞	hurt
保持，保有	現在式	keep
	過去式	kept
	過去分詞	kept
知道，認識	現在式	know
	過去式	knew
	過去分詞	known
放下，下蛋	現在式	lay
	過去式	laid
	過去分詞	laid
領導，領先	現在式	lead
	過去式	led
	過去分詞	led
學習，得知	現在式	learn
	過去式	learned, learnt
	過去分詞	learned, learnt

離開，遺留	現在式	leave
	過去式	left
	過去分詞	left
借出	現在式	lend
	過去式	lent
	過去分詞	lent
讓	現在式	let
	過去式	let
	過去分詞	let
躺，臥	現在式	lie
	過去式	lay
	過去分詞	lain
點燃，照亮	現在式	light
	過去式	lit, lighted
	過去分詞	lit, lighted
失去，輸掉，迷失	現在式	lose
	過去式	lost
	過去分詞	lost
做，使	現在式	make
	過去式	made
	過去分詞	made

可能，也許	現在式	may
	過去式	might
	過去分詞	×
意味，意指	現在式	mean
	過去式	meant
	過去分詞	meant
遇見，開會，認識	現在式	meet
	過去式	met
	過去分詞	met
弄錯，誤認	現在式	mistake
	過去式	mistook
	過去分詞	mistaken
誤會，曲解	現在式	misunderstand
	過去式	misunderstood
	過去分詞	misunderstood
付，支付	現在式	pay
	過去式	paid
	過去分詞	paid
證明	現在式	prove
	過去式	proved
	過去分詞	proved, proven

擺放，放置	現在式 put 過去式 put 過去分詞 put
放棄，辭職	現在式 quit 過去式 quit 過去分詞 quit
閱讀，讀懂	現在式 read 過去式 read 過去分詞 read
騎乘，搭坐	現在式 ride 過去式 rode 過去分詞 ridden
響，打電話	現在式 ring 過去式 rang 過去分詞 rung
升起，起床	現在式 rise 過去式 rose 過去分詞 risen
跑	現在式 run 過去式 ran 過去分詞 run

中文	形式	英文
說	現在式	say
	過去式	said
	過去分詞	said
看見，理解	現在式	see
	過去式	saw
	過去分詞	seen
尋求，尋找	現在式	seek
	過去式	sought
	過去分詞	sought
賣，販售	現在式	sell
	過去式	sold
	過去分詞	sold
送，寄送	現在式	send
	過去式	sent
	過去分詞	sent
設立，確定	現在式	set
	過去式	set
	過去分詞	set
震動，發抖，握手	現在式	shake
	過去式	shook
	過去分詞	shaken

將會	現在式	shall
	過去式	should
	過去分詞	×
閃耀，發亮	現在式	shine
	過去式	shone, shined
	過去分詞	shone, shined
射擊，發射	現在式	shoot
	過去式	shot
	過去分詞	shot
表現，展現	現在式	show
	過去式	showed
	過去分詞	shown, showed
關閉，停業	現在式	shut
	過去式	shut
	過去分詞	shut
唱歌	現在式	sing
	過去式	sang
	過去分詞	sung
沉沒，沉落	現在式	sink
	過去式	sank
	過去分詞	sunk

坐	現在式	sit
	過去式	sat
	過去分詞	sat
睡覺	現在式	sleep
	過去式	slept
	過去分詞	slept
滑動，滑落	現在式	slide
	過去式	slid
	過去分詞	slid
講話，說話	現在式	speak
	過去式	spoke
	過去分詞	spoken
超車，加速	現在式	speed
	過去式	sped, speeded
	過去分詞	sped, speeded
拼字	現在式	spell
	過去式	spelled, spelt
	過去分詞	spelled, spelt
花費，度過	現在式	spend
	過去式	spent
	過去分詞	spent

散播，延伸	現在式	spread
	過去式	spread
	過去分詞	spread
站立，忍受	現在式	stand
	過去式	stood
	過去分詞	stood
偷竊	現在式	steal
	過去式	stole
	過去分詞	stolen
戳，刺，卡住	現在式	stick
	過去式	stuck
	過去分詞	stuck
叮，螫	現在式	sting
	過去式	stung
	過去分詞	stung
打擊，攻擊	現在式	strike
	過去式	struck
	過去分詞	struck, stricken
發誓，罵髒話	現在式	swear
	過去式	swore
	過去分詞	sworn

中文	形式	英文
清掃，席捲	現在式	sweep
	過去式	swept
	過去分詞	swept
游泳	現在式	swim
	過去式	swam
	過去分詞	swum
搖擺，擺動	現在式	swing
	過去式	swung
	過去分詞	swung
拿，取	現在式	take
	過去式	took
	過去分詞	taken
教導	現在式	teach
	過去式	taught
	過去分詞	taught
撕開，撕裂，扯破	現在式	tear
	過去式	tore
	過去分詞	torn
告訴，說，顯示	現在式	tell
	過去式	told
	過去分詞	told

想，思考，認為	現在式	think
	過去式	thought
	過去分詞	thought
丟，投擲，舉行	現在式	throw
	過去式	threw
	過去分詞	thrown
懂，理解	現在式	understand
	過去式	understood
	過去分詞	understood
醒來，喚醒	現在式	wake
	過去式	woke
	過去分詞	woken
穿，戴	現在式	wear
	過去式	wore
	過去分詞	worn
弄溼	現在式	wet
	過去式	wet
	過去分詞	wet
將要，願意	現在式	will
	過去式	would
	過去分詞	×

贏，贏得	現在式	win
	過去式	won
	過去分詞	won
寫，寫信	現在式	write
	過去式	wrote
	過去分詞	written

就是這一本，超實用的旅遊英語

專為初學者設計
提供最實用的英語會話句子
一次搞定英語旅遊會話！
旅行不能忘記帶的英文小寶典！

馬上說，生活英文迷你短句

編輯了在家中時光，交通旅遊，飲食購物以及學校職場上的常用會話。

將英文從基本開始學起，並對各種情境加以解釋說明，從生活瑣事來活用英文。

讓你輕輕鬆鬆將英文脫口而出！

韓國人天天會用到的韓語單字

韓國人從早到晚一定會用到的詞彙，
不管是早晨梳洗、開車上班、用餐、
職場、學校、購物、玩樂、就醫等…
只要是你想知道、你想學的、所有最
生活化的韓語單字通通都在這一本。

韓國人天天會用到的韓語短句

想知道韓國人每天都一定會說什麼話嗎？
除了안녕하세요!之外
你還知道哪些常用短句呢？

一本在手
韓語常用短句絕對難不倒你!!

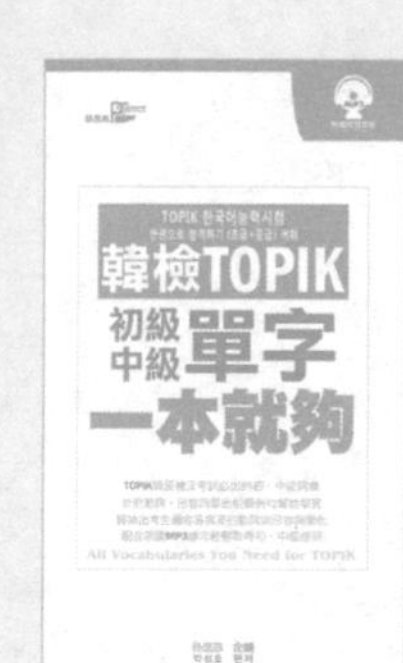

韓檢TOPIK單字一本就夠 初級+中級

本書整理出TOPIK韓語檢定考試必出的初、中級詞彙，針對動詞、形容詞舉出相關例句幫助學習，同時歸納出考生最容易搞混、出錯的動詞以及形容詞變化配合朗讀MP3加強聽力讓您輕輕鬆鬆取得韓語初、中級證照！

輕鬆學韓語：旅遊會話篇

你想去韓國自助旅行嗎？

最充實的旅遊會話、單字
通通都在這一本！

英語館 系列 04

最實用的國民生活英語單字書

臧琪蕾 

許純華 

林于婷

Parrot 語言鳥

出版社

22103 新北市汐止區大同路三段１８８號９樓之１
TEL （02）8647-3663
FAX （02）8647-3660

法律顧問 方圓法律事務所 涂成樞律師

總經銷：永續圖書有限公司
永續圖書線上購物網
www.foreverbooks.com.tw

CVS代理 美璟文化有限公司
TEL （02）2723-9968
FAX （02）2723-9668

出版日 2013年06月

國家圖書館出版品預行編目資料

最實用的國民生活英語單字書 / 臧琪蕾編著.
-- 初版. -- 新北市 : 語言鳥文化, 民102.06
面 ; 公分. -- (英語館 ; 4)
ISBN 978-986-88955-6-0(平裝附光碟片)
1.英語 2.詞彙
805.12 102006341

剪下後傳真、掃描或寄回至「22103新北市汐止區大同路3段188號9樓之1語言鳥文化收」

語言鳥 Parrot 讀者回函卡

最實用的國民生活英語單字書

感謝您對這本書的支持，請務必留下您的基本資料及常用的電子信箱，以傳真、掃描或使用我們準備的免郵回函寄回。我們每月將抽出一百名回函讀者寄出精美禮物，並享有生日當月購書優惠價，語言鳥文化再一次感謝您的支持與愛護！

想知道更多更即時的消息，歡迎加入"永續圖書粉絲團"

傳真電話：（02）8647-3660

電子信箱：yungjiuh@ms45.hinet.net

基本資料

姓名：＿＿＿＿＿＿ ○先生 ○小姐 電話：＿＿＿＿＿＿

E-mail：＿＿＿＿＿＿

地址：＿＿＿＿＿＿

購買此書的縣市及地點：＿＿＿＿＿＿

□連鎖書店 □一般書局 □量販店 □超商

□書展 □郵購 □網路訂購 □其他＿＿＿＿

您對於本書的意見

內容	：	□滿意	□尚可	□待改進
編排	：	□滿意	□尚可	□待改進
文字閱讀	：	□滿意	□尚可	□待改進
封面設計	：	□滿意	□尚可	□待改進
印刷品質	：	□滿意	□尚可	□待改進

您對於敝公司的建議

免郵廣告回信

221-03

基隆郵局登記證

基隆廣字第000153號

新北市汐止區大同路三段188號9樓之1

語言鳥文化事業有限公司

編輯部 收

請沿此虛線對折免貼郵票，以膠帶黏貼後寄回，謝謝！

語言是通往世界的橋梁

語言鳥 Parrot
語言是通往世界的橋梁

語言鳥 Parrot
語言是通往世界的橋梁